Introduction

There are a lot of great stories found in our history. In America, or anywhere else in the world, our lives ARE history. Some events are famous and remembered. Some SHOULD be remembered and sadly, are not. That's where Ray Stone History Stories come in.

History is important. We learn from history. It helps us repeat mistakes of the past, if we pay attention, but history is also fascinating and, if can be entertaining. We can learn so much about the past, the near past and from long-ago. It can help us appreciate our standing in life today, and what others may have done to help us right wrongs, live in freedom, enjoy our pastimes, and much more.

I have always wanted to bring a character like Ray Stone into my life. A highly intelligent teen. A teen I wished I could have been. One from an intelligent family. An imperfect young man but a man with, generally, a good moral compass. Trying to do the right thing. Taking his cues from his parents, from his knowledge of history, and from his own conscience, always talking to him.

Ray Stone lives in the real city of Athens, Georgia, in the year 1978. His father is a history professor, a generally serious, laid-back person that met Ray's mother while both were students at The University of Wisconsin. He is now a professor at the University of Georgia, and Ray is a high school senior. Ray's sister, Linda, is highly intelligent, a brilliant math student, and Ray's lovable adversary in life, as is often seen between siblings. They love each other, but never pass up the opportunity for a sassy remark or to outdo the other one.

I was also a teen living in Georgia in 1978, and the following year, attended the University of Georgia, but that's where the comparisons end. Ray is the young man I would have aspired to be, and my own love of history and of America serves as the basis of the stories, by I am not Ray, and can only dream of having his adventures.

Ray has been having vivid dreams that he is sent back in time. Sometimes to meet very famous people, or ordinary people in extraordinary times. Often, Ray is asked to listen to the tales, the problems, the concerns of their people. Their dreams, their dilemmas, their struggle and heartache. He is a bystander, in a frozen moment of time, and even Ray doesn't know if these dreams are actually real. How can they be, and yet, they are too real not to sometimes think otherwise.

The purpose of the Ray Stone series is to teach as well as to entertain. If you are entertained, that's great, but maybe you'll learn something new, and it will spur you to do your own research. I take a subject I know "something" about, but by the time I'm done, I know a lot more, and I always feel better about learning.

Dave Goren

Table Contents

Bravery at Bastogne

Ray Stone walked out of the parking lot at Stegeman Hall, at the University of Georgia. Stegeman was an older building next to Sanford Stadium, and it housed the swimming pool, basketball and weight rooms, the band room, and the campus police department. In the large parking lot, you could throw a rock and just about hit the bridge that passed right by the stadium scoreboard. Prime parking for games if there ever was one. This was where, on Friday before a Bulldogs home football game, you would see a lot full of campers and season-ticket holders who also earned the best parking spots in town. Ray also loved football, but this was a Friday, but not a Football weekend.

It was a nice April day in Athens, GA. The Bulldogs had finished a 9-2-1 schedule, winning a thriller against the hated Yellow Jackets of Georgia Tech, prevailing 29-28, but lost the final game against Stanford in the Astro Bluebonnet Bowl. Another good year, but always, the "what if" questions remain. It was 1978, and Ray figured the Dawgs were lucky to have a running back like Willie McClendon, one of the best since Frank Sinkwich, he was told. It was unlikely that Georgia would find anybody of McClendon's running talents anytime soon.

Raymond, Ray, to his friends and family, was the son of a history professor, and if there was anything he liked more than college football, it was history, which helped a lot, since he could speak to his Dad about almost anything having to do with history. He was making his way down Sanford Drive, past the bookstore, Memorial Hall, and across the street to Park Hall, where he was to meet up with his Dad.

His dad Gene was a calm and collected man who looked like the Professor he was. He had that well-to-do look, tweet jacket, patches and all, but looks were deceiving. Ray's grandpa, his dad's father, spent a career working at the "Yards", the Massive Union Stock Yards in Chicago, the "hog butcher to the world". This 475 acre site slaughtered millions upon millions of animals a year, and Ray's dad grew up in the nearby area called "Back of the Yards". Grandpa started small and worked to assume a managerial position, but they lived a humble life, and his grandfather was determined to give Ray's dad, and his sister Linda, a better life than him.

Gene studied hard and wound up getting an academic scholarship to the University of Wisconsin, about 150 miles away, in Madison. Only about three and half hours away by bus. Gene fell in love with Madison, the "city of four lakes", and became a die-hard Badgers fan. He eventually earned a PhD. in American History, and after two other positions, was offered a nice position on the staff at the Franklin College of Arts and Sciences at Georgia. Ray had already been born and was three when the family left the University of Wisconsin at Eau Claire, and headed way down south to Athens, GA.

The Stone family, Gene and Carol, Ray and Susan, settled into a nice life, and enjoyed another college town with so much to offer. Ray was now an 11th grader at Clarke Central High School, just down Baxter Street from the college campus. He figured he would attend Georgia, as the tuition would be lower. His dad would love nothing better than for him to be a Badger, but the in-state savings in Georgia couldn't be ignored.

Ray was a good student, a chip off the 'ole block when it came to history, but with a slightly more wild streak than his dad. Nothing to be alarmed about. There was time just six months earlier when Ray snuck out to attend a B52's concert at "The Last Resort" bar. The Athens group was already famous, touring the country, and the days of them being a local band were already gone, so Ray took advantage of the rare opportunity, and attended. Drank a lot, too, and his parents were not happy about it. It took a couple of licks that he knew he deserved, and they all moved on. His Dad really didn't like confrontation and if anyone doled out the punishment, it was Mom. In a couple of years he'd be of legal age, where groups like R.E.M. would be happy to entertain him at the 40 Watt Club and other venues.

"Dr. Gene" as many of his pupils called him, enjoyed teaching his classes. You could see the passion in his eyes as he challenged his students to dissect and analyze historical events in American history. He loved America because he felt he knew it, warts and all. Ray soaked it all in and Dr. Gene loved it.

Ray doesn't know when "the events" began to occur, as he called them. Maybe three years earlier. Anybody would simply dismiss them as dreams. After all, his Dad WAS a history Professor, and Ray loved the stories of American valor, struggle, victories as well as defeats. But the dreams were too real, and he would wake up with artifacts in his bed or a pocket that couldn't be explained. That was the kicker. But explaining it would raise red flags that Ray just didn't want to deal with. Definitely shrink territory, and Dr. Gene knew a couple. So, for the time being, he was keeping it to himself. He could always call them "vivid dreams" but there were simply too many unusual things involved with it. On top of that was the randomness of it all. It wasn't like he was watching a documentary on the Cuban Missel Crisis, then dreamed about it. They came out of nowhere. One night, he was on a trail with Lewis and Clark, another time, Mount Vernon. In 1798. There, he found the retired General Washington, walking with a one Dr. Jean-Pierre Le Mayeur. His dentist. Turns out his dentures were not made of wood, after all. Ray knows, because the General told him. How the hell could he explain that to his dad, or to anyone? He couldn't. Better to be thought crazy than erase all doubt, or something like that.

Ray walked through the picturesque North Campus, past the library, chapel, and past the iron Arch that marked the beginning of the campus and stopped off at the Varsity restaurant for a couple of chili dogs and a frosted orange drink, on the corner of Broad Street and College Avenue. The Varsity had TV rooms, so he killed some time before heading back to his car at the Stegman parking lot.

After finishing up some homework and catching an episode of Barney Miller, he headed for bed, just like most any night, but an "event" was soon to happen that would once again challenge Ray and shake him to the core.

Ray woke up to a huge explosion that made him feel that his eardrums were about to burst. A huge spray of dirt and mud flew up in every direction. He was on a street, mostly dirt. In a town, but where? He noticed solders running in several directions and another soldier grabbed him and shouted, "Get the hell down!", and he did just that. He kept his head down, but then looked up. More soldiers. A long line of narrow homes, several busted wide open. It was a war zone, but where? He heard English but mostly, chaos. Then, another voice, "Private, get the hell off the street". It was directed toward him. The skies were cloudy, smoke filled the air. He was wearing a uniform. There on the sleeve, was an American patch.

He got up and ran into a building across the street. He was terrified. He was having another event and felt like he was about to get his head blown off. The building he ran into seemed like some kind of schoolroom, although the desks were scattered around into a corner. "Hey, get that door shut!", came a sound from another soldier, sitting in the corner.

"Who the hell are you?, came the response from the soldier, with a rank of private. Ray looked to see that he had the same single stripe, and for the first time, saw his other shoulder, with the Screaming Eagle of the 101st Airborne Division. "Old Abe", thought Ray. There was always some kind of connection, however small, wasn't there?" The Eagle on this famous patch was named after the mascot of the The 8th Wisconsin Volunteer Infantry Regiment during the Civil War. It was a fitting emblem for a division that would crush its enemies by falling upon them like a thunderbolt from the skies. Old Abe was legendary in Wisconsin. He lived early right in Eau Claire, where his dad used to teach, and went into battle. The Confederates wanted badly to kill that bird, but he lived through the war, only to die several years later from the aftermath of a fire. His image is even depicted at Camp Randall Stadium, home of the Wisconsin Badgers, where Ray had been with his dad, for a game. It's still his Dad's team and he knew Old Abe as if he was alive during that time. Well, Old Abe was the inspiration for the Army's 101st Airborne Division, which was organized right in Milwaukee after being demobilized after the first World War. If only he could tell his Dad that he wore the patch of the 101st Airborne, however undeserved as he obviously was.

"Ray, Ray Stone". "Yeah, how you doin' Ray Stone", came the reply. "You old enough to be in this man's Army? Jesus, you look fifteen". Ray was seventeen but lied. Well, I'm nineteen". "Relax, just giving you the business". He put his hand out. "I'm John Dockery. Sergeant told me to find a place to sleep for the night. Holy mackerel, these Krauts are killing us. We were driving 'em right back to Berlin. They busted wide open, and they're everywhere". Ray was beginning to figure some of this out, but he's been in these situations and always put his foot in his mouth. He knew he had to keep things simple and vague. "Yeah, it's crazy". "Crazy ain't the word," Private Dockery said. Ray could make out a distinctive northeast accent of some kind. Of course, Ray's mild southern accent wouldn't be missed. "Where you from, Ray, other than down South? That much I can hear. Hadn't met any Southerners until I got down to Louisiana, at Claiborne." Dockery was referring to Camp Claiborne in central Louisiana, where more than a half million men trained from various units, from 1939 to 1946, including the 101st. "Let me tell you something. The heat down there was murder. I don't know how you guys can handle that all the time". "I'm from Athens, Georgia." Ray said. "No kidding", said John. "Never heard of it. Well, Southern boy, throw your gear down because we're stuck here for the night".

Ray was wet, cold, and hungry, and he had just gotten there. "John, anything to eat around here?" "I wish", said John. Nothing for tonight. Nothing in here. Here, have a Chesterfield. "No thanks", Ray said. "Don't smoke". "Don't smoke? You nuts?: John laughed. I'd lose my mind. I say "Smoke 'em if you got 'em", mimicking a popular ad campaign of the day. "Well, here, have a couple sticks of gum. It's Orbit. I like Chiclets better, but can't get 'em. You got any?" Ray decided to try and sound a little bit normal. "Nope, can't get Chiclets, lately" John said "Right, they're out. Here take a couple of sticks." Ray put a stick in his mouth and the other in his pocket, for later. "Hey, thanks, John."

"So John, where you from?" "Me, I'm from Weehawken, New Jersey, two blocks from the river. Nice views of the city. You can see the Empire State Building. Tallest building in the world. My dad worked on that site back in '30 and '31" said John proudly. "Tell you what, that job saved our family. I mean, I was about six, but the jobs were scarce, I tell you what". Ray knew that was only a year or so after the stock market crash of 1929. "Tell you what, I don't think they'll ever put up a taller building than the Empire State". John's clear admiration was a product of the work his dad was able to do, and that he could look out and see his Dad's handiwork, towering above the Manhattan skyline. "Bet they don't have anything like that in the South". "No, nothing much like that. We have a few taller buildings in Atlanta". "Atlanta", John said. "Don't know much about it." Ray had to be careful what he said. Atlanta was still nothing like New York, though he had to remember not to mention the 70-story Peachtree Plaza, at the time, the world's tallest hotel, because that glass and steel building went up only two years earlier, in 1976. "Well, compared to New York, it's pretty small". "Damn right", John said. He was proud of his neighboring city. He gazed ahead, and then repeated quietly, "Tallest building in the world".

"So, how old are you, again?" John asked, but without waiting for an answer, continued, "Me, I'm nineteen. Finished high school and was training to be an auto mechanic. "Hey, I could put in a new (Buick) Roadmaster engine in no time", but now look at us. Hey, John said, you like sports? Me, I'm a baseball man. 2nd team all-state catcher from Weehawken High. New school opened in '40. Now, as far as my favorites, I'm a Yanks man all the way. Another World Series win in '40. Nobody like the Yanks. Now, I know DiMaggio is the big man on the Yankees, but see, I'm a catcher, so my favorite is Bill Dickey". John realized something, "Hey, he's a southern guy like you. Alabama, or Arkansas, something like that. It's all the same to me. Met him once, too". Finally, John took a breath and let Ray speak, even though Ray was happy to let him go on. "Who do you like?" John asked. "Well, I'm more of a college football fan, but my dad's from Chicago and follows the Cubs." "The Cubs?" John laughed. "Dem Cubbies got nothing, sorry. Losing season in '40, I know that much, and as far as football, hey I like it just fine. The (New York) Giants have a helluva team, or they did, but your old man should be happy. The (Chicago) Bears beat my Giants in the championship game of '41, but you know, they won it in '38. Yeah, I like football just fine, but me, like I said, I'm a baseball man". It was turning out that Ray didn't need to say to much except agree. Private John Dockery was happy to control the conversation, as blasts continued outside, both men trying to ignore what might happen if a shell landed on top of them. Ray took a small chance just to keep Private Dockery happy "Yeah, those Giants had have been good the last few years". "Yeah, you ain't kidding, but like I said, I'm a baseball man". This was getting a little monotonous.

Even the Germans, by now, would know that John Dockery was a baseball man.

Suddenly, a loud explosion shook the building. Something fell very close by. The walls shook. It shook John enough for him to stop talking about himself and the Yanks. "Holy mackerel", that was close.

"Looks like we'll never get any shut-eye tonight, Ray". On that, Ray could agree. "So tell me, did you drop in near Utah, or in Belgium? Without any hesitation, or waiting for a reply (Ray could see that he wouldn't have to say much, thankfully) John went on. "I came in during (Operation) Market Garden". "Oh yeah, me, too". Dockery said "Yeah, thought so". Ray dodged that. "Well that didn't go the way we had hoped, but we did get a couple of bridges blown up. Anyway, hell of a way to celebrate Christmas, huh?" "Oh, yeah, it's Christmas. Yeah, that stinks", Ray said. "No, it's tomorrow" said Dockery. "You're a little shell-shocked, but can't blame you". Ray faked a laugh and said "I can't remember anything anymore, even Christmas". That worked. "Yeah, just hoping to survive, right? I know exactly what you mean. Hey, I got a job waiting for me when I get out of here, right in Hoboken. My Uncle's place". John finally thought of Ray, "Bet I guess you never heard of Hoboken, just like I never heard of Athens, Georgia". But Ray did know some interesting trivia, although he didn't know how he knew it. He wanted to sound cool, to match Dockery's style. "Everybody knows Hoboken. That's Sinatra's town". "Holy mackerel!" Dockery said, almost a shout. "Not bad, Stone. My dad was in the fire department with Frank's dad. We actually saw Dorsey's band once. It was really something." Ray couldn't remember Dorsey. He was more interested in the B52s, Love Tractor, R.E.M., and the Atlanta Rhythm Section, but he had more or less figured out John Dockery by now. John wanted to talk, not listen. "Hey, that really IS something!" Ray said. "Yeah, no kiddin'". So now, without saying too much and blowing his "cover", Ray was accepted by John. In this environment, everybody needs somebody to talk to. Ray, too, because he was never really sure how much was real and what wasn't, but the freezing Belgium winter felt about as real as it was going to get, except for the noise of war, which was scaring the hell of him.

Ray seemed to doze off, in spite of it all, but only for a few minutes, he thought. He wasn't sure. "Hey, how do you sleep during all of this?" Dockery said. "Anyway, like I was sayin', we're almost out of ammo and we're still encircled. They say Patton's on the way, but we're not sure. So the Germans got us surrounded and sends in a couple of Krauts to demand our surrender to ole' General McAuliffe. They say 'surrender, or else', or something like that. You hear about that?" Ray knew he would only have to feed John his next line, "I've been hearing something like that, yeah", Ray said. "Exactly. Can you imagine? Well, I know you heard the General said 'nuts'." John starts laughing out loud and then actually acts out the scene, first with a terrible German accents "American, surrender or else. Oh yea? Go tell your General I said "Nuts"! Ray took a little liberty. "Sounds just like the General, doesn't it?" "And how", John said. They both laughed. Dockery from the General's comments and Ray, just glad to see a little relief during their dire situation.

John went on, pontificating about the world, "Yeah, these Germans. Hell, I AM German, on my mom's side, anyway. Still probably got relatives there. Got a cousin who knows a guy that was on the '36 Olympic team, you know?" Ray didn't know that but listened. Not that he had much of a choice. "So, anyway, we're reading about the Nazi's, how they hate Jews and most anybody else not just like them, but my cousin's friend comes back and says that everything was fine. Nothing was said. Everything was spotless and clean, and the people were so friendly. Flags everywhere. Stinkin' Nazi Flags". Ray didn't want to go into any details, all he knew about the camps, still not well-known at this point, but he was now a little curious, and put out a comment, a feeler. "Well, that was for show. They were up to something". "Yeah, damned right. They were up to this. But why? I mean, we, Americans and others, we were here like, twenty-five years ago. Why the hell should we keep coming back?" Here's where Ray could teach John a thing or two, but he didn't see the benefit of giving John a history lesson, like Dr. Gene would be doing. He could do some of his own pontificating, like how the Treaty of Versailles caused a crippling effect on the German economy, sowing the seeds of resentment that allowed a man like Hitler to gain power. This was a little above the interest, and maybe the comprehension of a certain Private Dockery. But he knew how to stay on his good side, and that was agreeing with him. "Well, Ray said to Dockery, I guess they wanted more". That was a good setup for a predictable John Dockery response. "Well, they're getting' it, ain't they?", said Dockery, as the men were part of a town encircled by elite German troops, but that would change.

"I don't get them, and their ideology", said Dockery, Ray being surprised at his use of the word, and the elevated level, suddenly, of discussion. I mean, I don't know a lot of Jewish kids in Weehawken. I played little league with a Bobby Greenberg. Nice kid, didn't cause a lick of trouble, but he moved away somewhere before I got into high school. I mean, I don't get it." The conversation didn't go any further on this, and Ray was glad, so John simply moved on.

"So, Sarge says we got some additional ammo dropped in by C-47s, and it looks like I'll be headin' out to the perimeter in a few hours". Dockery was referring to the perimeter around the outskirts of Bastogne, where the 101st was desperately trying to hold off the German Panzer Units. So far, these brave men, cold, and with little to no food or medical supplies, were still holding out, while Patton's Third Army was moving at top speed to try and break the encirclement, coming from Assenois, to the Southwest.

Then, there was quiet. For over an hour. Finally, John Dockery dozed off. Ray sat there, thinking how any kid a year out of chasing bobby-sockers and learning how to fix cars was fighting for his life. This man, this kid, deserved to get out of here, go back to Wee-Haven, or whatever it was called, be a mechanic, find a nice girl, and have a family.

It was a week and a day since 410,000 German soldiers began their offensive, known as the Ardennes Counteroffensive, but better known as the Battle of the Bulge. Bastogne was right at the heart of it, and it would be another month or so until the Germans could be pushed back to their original lines. It was possibly the last major offensive of the War, and the Allies continued pushing east, over the Rhine and meeting up with the Soviet forces, three months later, on April 25th, on the Elbe River, a symbolic but important moment, a sign of the end for the Third Reich, though the beginning of an increased animosity between what would be the two superpowers for the next forty years, the United States and the Soviet Union. In fact, the Germans had to surrender twice, on May 7th and again on May 9th, once to the Western Allies, and the second time, to the

Soviets. But at last, the war, at least on this side of the globe, would be over. The Japanese would be another story.

"Hey, let's go", a head entered into the doorway. Dockery, follow me. He didn't know Ray and didn't address him. Dockery shook Ray's hand, and was genuinely sincere, "Hey, thanks for keeping me company. It helped, and tell your old man to give up on those Cubbies. They'll never be champs." Ray smiled and said "Sure, John. You take care of yourself" as Private John Dockery headed out the door. Ray closed his eyes as things went Stone, his body suddenly warmed up, and as he opened his eyes, he recognized his bedroom, the alternating Georgia Bulldogs and Wisconsin Badgers pennants on the wall. The sun was up, but he didn't know the day or anything else.

"Hey, sleepyhead", came a response. A wonderful sound. It was his Mom, Carol. "It's Saturday but you can still get up and do something productive, you know? It's 10:00 already". She said it with a smile. It WAS Saturday, after-all. "Oh, wow, I didn't realize. Yeah, I'm getting up." "Wish I could have such a great night's sleep" said his Mom. If she only knew. "Oh, one other thing. I grabbed your shirt early this morning that you threw on the floor, and put it in the wash. Did you leave a stick of gum in there? It was extremely messy to clean up. You need to be more careful about that kind of thing."

John Dockery would survive Bastogne, although he lost a toe, a condition that would plague him for the rest of his life, but not from having a good life. He married an on-again, off-again girlfriend right from Weehawken, and went to work in his Uncle's garage for ten years. He and his wife had three kids, all healthy, and at fifty-seven, he became a Grandfather to one, and eventually, to five grandchildren. He eventually opened up his own garage in Clifton, NJ, and one of his sons took it over for him. Another son attended Yale, and then medical school, and a third son, an accountant. John had made it, but didn't talk much at all about his wartime experiences. He wondered once or twice about a certain Ray Stone, but then again, he met a lot of guys that were there one moment and gone the next. He didn't want to think much about the Georgia boy who was too dumb to light-up a cigarette when he had the chance. John died of lung cancer at the age of eighty-two, in 2006.

He probably never thought he'd be alive to see the 21st century, let alone see another town outside of Bastogne.

The Question of Independence

It was late June, and school was out in sunny Athens, GA. It was 82 degrees. It would get hotter. As a Professor's son, Raymond Stone, Ray to his friends and family, was able to hang out at Legion Pool, the outdoor pool at the University of Georgia, swim, and look at the "scenery". Even though the campus thinned out considerably during the summer, there were still more than enough pretty girls to look at, at the pool and around town, even if he were still in high school, and they probably wouldn't give him the time of day. Well, he could look.

He had a summer job, flipping burgers, bussing tables, washing dishes, and whatever else was needed, at Allen's Bar & Grill in what residents all called the "Normaltown" section of Athens. The Navy Supply School was within walking distance, and they helped make Allen's somewhat famous, by wearing the Allen's t-shirt in different ports around the world. They had good food and good music, and some of the local legends of rock and roll would come by. But Ray got his job because his dad frequented the place for their burgers and got into a conversation with the owner. His dad liked to say "I like Allen's Burgers. It's not quite Dotty Dumpling's Dowry, in Madison, but it's the best they've got in Athens. Well, anyway, he came home and said that he could probably work at Allen's, once Ray met the owner, and he did need a job, so off he went. He got one meal after four hours, and he worked about twenty-five hours a week. Enough to make a little spending money but not so many hours where he couldn't get into a little bit of trouble around town.

July 4th was coming up and they were going to go boating with his parent's friends and their family, on Lake Lanier, only about forty miles away. After boating, they would go eat and then watch fireworks. It was going to be a long but good day. School at Clarke Central High would be great in the fall, his senior year. He was going to go through the motions of applying to colleges, but likely, he would stay right in Athens. He could do better, perhaps, but he could do worse. Wisconsin was still an option, and his dad would be ecstatic. His Mom went there, too. That's where his parents met, but she didn't display the "rah-rah", school spirit that his dad did. How many times would he have to suffer his dad waking him up to the strains of "On Wisconsin?":

"On, Wisconsin! On, Wisconsin! Plunge right through that line!
Run the ball right down the field, a touchdown sure this time.
On, Wisconsin! On, Wisconsin! Fight on for her fame,
Fight! Fellows! Fight! Fight, fight, we'll win this game.
On, Wisconsin! On, Wisconsin! Stand up, Badgers sing!
'Forward' is our driving spirit loyal voices ring.
On, Wisconsin! On, Wisconsin! Raise her glowing flame
Stand, fellows, let us now salute her name!"

Gene Stone thought it was funny with the music blaring in the background. Ray did not. Gene was normally a quiet man, but every so often, he would get a "wild hair" when he was in a good mood, and thought it was funny to wake up Ray in this manner. If he thought Ray would attend Wisconsin, disturbing his sleep wasn't the way to go about it!

July 4th was great. It was the summer, there was no school, there were fireworks and boating, the girls wore bathing suits and short shorts, and his Dad got all caught up in the history. Well, that's what he did, and there's no denying that there would be no nation without an Independence Day.

It would be a long day on the 4th, but without any work for two days, he hung out with two of his friends, looking at magazines at Barnett's News Stand on College Avenue, a couple slices of pizza from Express Pizza and Pub a block from the Georgia campus, and then they called it a night.

He probably got into bed at around 11:30, about his average time but a little earlier than normal for a summer night. Watched a little Tonight Show with Johnny Carson. Naturally, so close to a holiday, Johnny wasn't there, but Joan Rivers was the guest host, with the Smothers Brothers, Bob Hope, and Joan Embrey, who brought on her usual selection of unusual animals. At some point, Ray fell into a deep sleep.

Ray opened his eyes, and wobbly, he found himself on a dirt road. It was hot, though nothing he didn't experience in Athens. He knew right away he had been taken to another place, at another time. "Quick, Ray, get your bearings." This time, it didn't take long. There, 100 feet away or so, past a horse and carriage, was a building he had already been inside more than once, on one of many historical jaunts his dad took him on. It was the Pennsylvania State House. The sun was far west in the sky, but it was still bright out. It felt like summer and the sun would set later. His guess was that it was about 7:00 P.M. He looked over himself. His clothing. He was wearing a jacket, breeches, high socks. In the summer? "Yes, Ray, you are dressed for the times, as always." He was becoming somewhat of an expert in the ways of fashion, to be prepared. Not something he would normally care about. He preferred a t-shirt with a Bulldog or rock group, shorts, on the short side, calf-length socks, and Converse All-Stars, just like his favorite player, Rick Barry of the Golden State Warriors.

He was heading for the State House, he knew that, instinctively, but what would he find? The Continental Congress? He couldn't face those delegates. He was just a kid. "Whoever is doing this? Why? If it's a dream, tell me! It just feels too real!" He had no choice. It always ended, but would today be like all the other days, or was it night? He had no choice. He had to see it through.

He walked past a man and woman. He gave a slight bow. It seemed to work. The woman smiled slightly. The man looked at him with some suspicion, but he was, after all, a man escorting a lady in whatever year he didn't yet know, except that it was some colonial period.

He approached the building, perhaps the tallest in Philadelphia, with its wooden steeple. It looked quite different than the building he visited just three years prior. Well, two years prior to 1978, the Bi-Centennial year, when his family went on the "trip of all trips", Philadelphia, Charlottesville, and Washington D.C. It was event after event. And crowded. Ray, even know-too-much-for-his-own-good Ray, didn't realize that much of the outside building, including the steeple and clock, were replaced in 1781 and again in 1828. Still, it was impressive, and he figured out what it was.

There was a front door. Of course, there is always a front door. But he was nervous. It could be worse. He has awoken in war zones. Here, it was very peaceful. For now. He sensed he had to enter that building.

He turned the knob and moved inside the wooden door. It was quite dark inside. No electrical ceiling lights. That's for sure. He did see several candles lit. The Argand lamp was introduced to Thomas Jefferson in Paris in 1784, but Ray was still trying to pin down this "event". It wouldn't take long.

Just a few feet away sat a man, face in hands, deep in thought but not looking very happy. The man looked up. Oh, no.

He had seen enough paintings. Wow, those artists were good. Too good. He didn't need a Polaroid. It was John Adams.

The 41-year-old delegate from the Commonwealth of Massachusetts, looked up, and studied Ray. Ray was seventeen and didn't look any older. He hoped that in the 1700's, he might be afforded a little more leeway. A little more respect. That wasn't to be, and certainly not with a future President. "Okay, Ray, please! Be careful. Mr. Adams will not know Rick Barry or Coach Dooley, or even Coach Dave McCain."

"Excuse me, young man, can you tell me exactly what you are doing in this hall?", Mr. Adams remarked, somewhat annoyed. Well, I'm sorry, I was looking for somebody" Ray was terrified that he would appear like alien, using words that won't match with the vocabulary of the time. "Whom, exactly, would you be looking for right here, and at this time, young man?" Okay, Ray, keep it simple. "My father told me he had a meeting here, but he didn't tell me whom it was with."

"Why, are you Mr. Adams?" asked Ray. He knew it had to be. "Why", asked the depressed-looking Delegate. "Do you want to admonish me as well?" Ray came up with something, "Admonish? Oh no, sir. My father admires you greatly." Adams replied, "Well, maybe he can have a seat in this cursed Congress. Where are you, and your father from?" Careful, Ray, maybe Athens, GA isn't the best answer. "I am from Savannah, Georgia, Mr. Adams." "Ah yes, Georgia. Mr. Walton, Dr. Hall, and Mr. Gwinnett. Good men. Patriots." Adams managed a weak smile, "You don't look much younger than George Walton. Indeed, George Walton was one of the youngest members of the Congress, at twenty-seven years of age.

Adams, while clearly aggravated at something, probably many things, suddenly decided to have a little bit of fun with the young man whom he had decided was educated. "So, tell me young man, where do YOU stand on the question of Independence?" Wow. Ray was astounded. Just astounded. John Adams was asking him to pontificate on the question of Independence! Ray could answer. "Well, sir, I am in favor of it. Whole-heartedly. We must be a free nation. We can no longer suffer under the rule of Britain. We have no representation and…."

"Indeed. Well, perhaps you can tell some of our more stubborn, insolent members of our distinguished Congress your sentiments. Naturally, we must be independent. The time has long passed."

"Even if it means war", added Ray, who now stepped over the line. "My good man", chided Adam's, we ARE at war! We have BEEN at war. Perhaps along the shores of your beloved Georgia, you do not feel the sting of it, but I can assure you that the blood is flowing along the Massachusetts Bay. Have the events of Lexington and Concord not yet reached your southern paradise? It was a year this April, and it is now the first of July." There was an uncomfortable silence. So, this was the passionate and sometimes disliked man who would become the nation's 2nd President." At least he knew the exact date, now. It was July 1st, 1776. About two weeks since Richard Henry Lee of Virginia called for the colonies' independence from Great Britain leading to the United States Declaration of Independence.

"Young man, I apologize to you." Adams said softly. "Clearly, my sentiments are a reflection of circumstances that you have not caused." Ray so badly wanted to have a real conversation. To discuss what he already knew, to possibly even reassure this great man that the nation would see its birth, and thrive, but he had already stepped over the line." It's quite alright, Mr. Adams. I'm certain the stresses of leadership have taken its toll on many a man". "Indeed", said John Adams, "though I am not in a position to complain. The Continental Army is in a constant shortage of supplies, and Abigail has been left alone during these tumultuous days. We have four children. She hasn't been quite the same since we lost Susanna eight years ago. The strain of running a home like that is too great a task. We write each often, in fact, constantly, but it is not the same. It does not replace personal contact. Let's not forget, we Colonies are property of King George III. He is not; and will not, take lightly to any notions of Independence". Adams said. Ray, himself now passionate, went for broke. "And yet we must achieve it. We must declare it for the world to hear!". Adams looked shocked. "Yes, young man. Indeed, we must", he said slowly, quietly. "But we must declare it in solidarity. The colonies must be in agreement, but allegiances remain. Stubbornness persists. Blindness is still on display among our fellow brethren." He added, under his breath. Damn them".

Could John Adams discuss this document, this weapon of war now perhaps in its 80th revision, with a boy that is even perhaps an agent of the British? A spy? Adams couldn't believe it. There was something innocent yet very different in this young man from Georgia. He saw. He knew. He was a patriot. Perhaps we weren't doomed after all. Not if there were others like him. "I wish Rutledge and Dickinson could hear from our youth, could understand that we must put aside petty differences, and unite as one. The enemy is across that vast body of water, marching against us, crushing our freedom. But we WILL be a land of freedom, where a government serves the people, abides by its wishes, a government by the people." "And OF the people", said Ray. He couldn't resist. "How old are you again?" Adams asked again?" "Seventeen, sir" said Ray, realizing that he may know too much for his own good. "But all men are created equal." Adams now, in his excitement, reading from the text. He had seen and rehearsed nothing but this text for days. "Careful, Ray. Do NOT start reciting the darned thing or you just MIGHT be labeled a spy." Ray thought "It was self-evident". He simply added. He simply said, "All men have basic rights." "Ray, whatever you do, he thought to himself, don't say 'inalienable'." He doubted the average man uttered that word, at that time, or any other. "Yes, yes", added Adams. "All men ARE created equal" Adams again uttered. "Free men or otherwise. If you understand, others across the land surely will."

During a break in conversation, Ray, hoping to gain as much real-life education as he could, asked "is Dr. Franklin here?" A slight smile broke across Adams' mouth. "Ah, the eminent Dr. Franklin. The polymath, the printer, the Postmaster General, philosopher, inventor, musician, scientist, and whatever other accolades have been awarded to him." You, and the world, wish to be in the great man's company. "Well,", said Ray, "my father has taught me much about him. He's a great man". "Naturally", said Adams. "On that, he would agree with you. But I forgive him for his excesses of knowledge and sarcasm. He's really a Boston man, you know. He is, no doubt, somewhere in the vicinity, although by now, possibly tucked away in his bed. Most likely, if he is awake, he is hobbling around with his gout. If you do see him, do not make mention of his son". Franklin's illegitimate son, William, the Royal Governor of New Jersey, was a Loyalist, and not at all warm to the cause of Independence. Adams obviously had great respect for Franklin, as did people in the Colonies, and in Great Britain, where he had lived most of the last twenty years or so. Yet, there was also some tension in Adams' voice. Perhaps there were some tensions in that association. Ray did not press further.

"My father has met Mr. Rutledge, while visiting Charleston, from Savannah". Ray planted a seed here. I assume you are referring to Edward and not John?", asked Mr. Adams. "Oh, yes", said Ray, now unsure. "Yes" said Adams, "the young South Carolina delegate. He, along with Mr. Dickinson of Pennsylvania, the thorns in my flesh." We will win him over, yet. Edward Rutledge did indeed sign the Declaration in just three days. Dickinson did not.

 "Young man", Adams said, "You have stumbled into this place at an appropriate time. You have injected some hope into this weary soul. I thank you for it".

Adams realized that he had spoken more than he had wished, and to a boy. Spoken, indeed. But he was touched. This boy, Adams thought, must have a great teacher in his father. Ray, for his part, felt a mixture of jubilance and fear. Away from his family, too far to travel between the great cities at this time. What could Ray say to console him? Tell him about jet airplanes? An hour and a half from Boston to Philadelphia. He'd be locked up for certain. "Mr. Adams, I believe we will break free from Great Britain, and become a great Republic, a nation of free citizens able to determine their own destiny, and you will help lead our nation." Adams stopped and looked hard at Ray. "Well, young man, I share your desires if not your expectations. We must first make unanimous our voices, and we are not there. Not yet." Ray wished he could tell him that he would have his unanimity in three short days." Well, sir, I should go. I wish there something I could do. Perhaps a little rum would be a good day to end the evening." "Adams was known to like his drink and forced a smile. "Or perhaps hard cider," Mr. Adams said.

"Ray began to walk away, toward the door." "Oh, young man, there is something you can do, for our Congress, for the Colonies, for all of us. Even for myself". "Yes, sir, what would that be?" Ray asked.

"Pray", Mr. Adams said.

Ray left. It was now dark. He walked toward the river and sat on the bank. He closed his eyes. Discussing the fate of the nation was exhausting.

He woke up staring at the Wisconsin Badger pennant on his wall. It was July 4th. He had to get up. The family was heading to the lake in 30 minutes. He got up to use the bathroom, but the door was locked. "Linda, hurry up! We're going to be late to the lake!" After several long minutes, the door sprang open, and Linda said to Ray, "Okay, okay, you can have it now! Jeez, what's up your butt?" Ray, still not quite back, looked at her incredulously, and said "Indeed!".

On July 4th, 56 Delegates of the Second Continental Congress signed the Declaration of Independence. The Declaration justified the independence of the United States. listing 27 colonial grievances against King George III and by asserting certain natural and legal rights, including a right of revolution. The Declaration holds one of the most powerful and famous words in American history:

"We hold these truths to be self-evident, that all men are created equal, that they are endowed by their Creator with certain unalienable Rights, that among these are Life, Liberty and the pursuit of Happiness."

The Revolutionary War would continue until October of, 1781, when British General Charles Cornwallis surrendered at Yorktown, ending the British will to fight, but it would be another two years, September 3, 1783, with the signing of the Treat of Paris, that formal terms and acceptance of American Independence became a reality. The fighting spread to Canada, to the southern colonies, and even to Spanish Louisiana.

The signers of the Declaration were learned men of different backgrounds and some different ideologies, who came together, often reluctantly, to sign this article of freedom. Thomas Jefferson, the Declaration's author, ultimately made eighty-six revisions, and shortening its length by a quarter.

The signers of the Declaration of Independence sacrificed for what the British considered an act of treason. While only a handful of signers are well-known, like John Adams, Thomas Jefferson, John Hancock, with his elaborate, large, and defiant signature, many others suffered greatly for the patriotism. Several were captured, driven into bankruptcy and ruin, their homes and families destroyed. Nine of fifty-six died during the war, from injuries and mistreatment. These were men who had a vision, a goal of a nation where a government served the people, and a nation that was founded on the concept of freedom and liberty.

Prelude to a Tragedy

Ray got up, slowly. Typical for a Monday. A September Monday in the fall of 1978. It was a good weekend, but it was never fun to go back to school, even though Ray, for all his fake portrayal as a "bad boy" at times, was an "A" student, as if his parents, and especially his Professor father, would accept anything less. That Saturday, the 'Dawgs beat the Baylor Texas Bears, 16-14. Nobody knew much about Baylor, a Texas team from the Southwest conference. All a Georgia fan knew was that after three straight losses to end the '77 season, to Florida, Auburn, and worst of all, Georgia Tech, any win was good. What Ray didn't know was that Baylor was on its way to a 3-8 season, while Georgia was to have a good year, at 9-2-1, but rarely that season when all the pieces would fit together. The "Bulldog nation" would have to wait three more years for that. Meanwhile, his dad's team, the Wisconsin Badgers, won a squeaker against Richmond (who?), but again, a win was a win in college football, and his dad was in good spirits. Ray would help his Dad celebrate at the breakfast table by donning his red Badgers shirt. He had preferred to wear a new shirt that he loved, a t-shirt of the great soul singer, James Brown, singing, with the words "Dooley's Junkyard Dogs", a hit single, at least with Georgia fans, celebrating the vaunted UGA defense, the "Junkyard Dogs". Brown, the "Godfather of Soul" was born in South Carolina, but nobody really needed to dwell on that. That was the home to the Clemson Tigers and South Carolina Gamecocks. Georgia fans didn't care for either school too much, but they didn't hate them nearly as much as they hated each other. James Brown was noted for being raised in Augusta, Georgia, and was a big football fan. Few could sing or dance like James Brown. Fans loved his music and his song dedicated to the Dawgs, but sometimes, Ray couldn't understand what the heck the man was saying. There was a part that said, "and a great man, in Joules". Who is Jolese, for God's sake? It took a few years before Ray saw the lyrics, and realized that Brown was referring to Joel Eaves, the Georgia Athletic Director, but even more famous at Auburn University, where he played several sports and was a winning coach. Still, he hired Vince Dooley, another Auburn man, but very good for Georgia. But where was the Junkyard Dogs t-shirt? There was no time to look. Time to eat and get out the door for school.

Ray didn't have to look much longer for his shirt. He reached the kitchen table. There's dad, in his tweet jacket, Mr. history professor, his Mom, Carol, and then Linda. Yes, Linda, wearing a strangely familiar shirt. "Linda, what the hell are you doing wearing my James Brown shirt". "Oh, relax, Ray", Linda said. "I needed a shirt, and there it was. I'm surprised you had something clean." "Well," Ray, smirked, "nobody told you that you could wear it. Mom, what the hell?"" Alright", Carol said, trying to keep the peace. "It's just a shirt, but next time, Linda, ask." "Fine, whatever". Linda rolled her eyes. Linda took the opportunity to drag Ray into a little trouble, if she could. "At least I wasn't at Papa Joe's Saturday night". Ray didn't know how she knew that Ray walked into the beer and peanuts dive on Baxter Street, near the high school and just a block or two from Brumby, the all-female hi-rise dorm that marked the western edge of the Georgia campus. "I only went in there to play Space Invaders". His Mom said nothing, and his dad gave him a fake, nasty look. "Be careful", his dad said. Ray knew his dad felt obligated to say something, even if it was half-hearted. What are you going to do about a high school senior with straight A's that has a beer once in a while? Ray was on the straight and narrow, considering he lived in the shadows of a school ranked both in football and on the list of "top party schools". "And you", Gene Stone said, directing his phony anger at Linda, "Don't be a tattletale". Linda smiled. Dad was a paper tiger, and puddy in the hands of his daughter. It was a good, loving, strong family. A little sarcasm and tension weren't a deal-breaker in this family. Anyway, what's a shirt?

School that day, the third week in, wasn't very exciting. There was no homework on Friday, though he'd get some today. No history classes his senior year. He had already taken everything available. His dad had selected three books for Ray. Two on the eastern front of World War Two, about Stalingrad and Leningrad, since Ray had read about everything he could get his hands on, on the Pacific Theater of War. There were always stories, military battles and then, personal stories of tragedy and sacrifice. Bombings, life in a war-torn area. Terror-filled skies, firebombed cities where people were sucked in. Dresden, Germany and the incendiary fires that literally sucked the air out all-around people. It was fascinating but terrible, Ray knew that. He had seen war, though nobody would ever believe it. Never, and it had to stay that way. That in itself was a terrible secret to keep. Even his dad wouldn't know. Couldn't know. Maybe someday. Afterall, anybody could have a dream, but Ray thought it was more, and that's where the discussion started and ended. He'd have to live through it. He always came back. The events ended, at least for him, but if were to believe the reality, it didn't end for those in these dreams. Ray walked out of it, woke up. Escaped, but if he were to believe his own senses, the others did not. They could not necessarily escape. There was nothing Ray could do, and he had to always "cover his bases". Blend in.

A couple of weeks went by. A nice win against the Clemson Tigers, but the Dawgs couldn't escape South Carolina without a loss somewhere, which came the week after, at Williams-Brice Stadium, to the Gamecocks. It wasn't really even close. Another disappointment. Maybe the Ole Miss Game back in Athens this Saturday would have a better result. Ray went back to sleep on a Wednesday night after finishing up some homework and catching 30 minutes of The Tonight Show. Johnny made a joke at the expense of Jimmy Carter, as if Georgia hadn't had a tough-enough week.

Ray awoke on his feet, and that could only mean one thing. He tried to clear his senses. Where was he now? He was walking. It was a park but not a very large one, and not far away he saw buildings. Several buildings, but suddenly, he saw a large object right in the park. It was an arch. He hoped he wasn't in Paris or a foreign country. He walked up to the white structure. There was a fountain. He looked up and saw an eagle in the center, high above, and then the inscription which spelled out, literally, what the arch was, and where Ray stood.

"Let us raise a standard to which the wise and the honest can repair. The event is in the hand of God"

Ray had been here. With his family, but at a different time. The horses and carriages moving along the street told him that right away. He was in New York's Washington Square Park, but when? He also saw cars that he had seen mostly in pictures, a Ford, a Matheson, a Kirsch Delivery Wagon, but Ray wasn't really a car guy, so to speak. Was it 1920? Maybe earlier. Lots of horse-drawn wagons still, but after 1910. Ray was pretty good at this but not great. He would have to continue walking and figure something out.

Most importantly, *why* was he here? There was always a reason of some kind.

He turned to his right, where there were some nice, shady trees, and continued to walk. He glanced at his body; he was dressed better than he thinks he has ever seen himself. What in the world was this? For one, he had a stick in this hand. A cane? No, a walking stick. He was wearing a double-breasted jacket, a vest, pants turned up at the cuff, a tie, and a hat. There was also a chain wrapped around a button. He followed the chain with his fingers, and in a pocket was a watch. A pocket watch. Goodness. On it was the name Elgin. It was 11:15 AM, even Ray could tell time the old-fashioned way. He was a regular dapper gentleman, but he didn't know why. He would certainly fit in, though he wasn't sure of the date, still. That wasn't the kind of thing you could ask, fancy threads or not.

He continued his walk across the street, blending in quite well, he thought. He was in the middle of the campus of New York University, NYU, more or less, and knew that Greenwich Village was in the vicinity.

Ray passed a building that looked to be around ten stories high and sitting on the stoop below was a young girl, perhaps fifteen. "Hey mister" she said. Could you tell me the time?" "Okay Ray", he thought. There are horse and buggy's, but also cars. Early 20th century. Probably not 1900 and probably not 1920. Maybe 1910 to 1915? He really didn't need to know just yet. Maybe it will come out in conversation. "Yes. It is fifteen minutes past eleven". He tried to be careful of any slang, as usual, but he'd been caught in far earlier times. "Thanks, Mister", came the reply. The girl had a slight accent, the kind from somebody who had once lived somewhere else, but now lived here. "Are you having a good day, young lady?" Ray had to think of something. She looked like a working-class girl, which might be to Ray's advantage. "Am I having a good day? Get a gander at you! All gussied up!" Ray said, "Yes, I suppose so. What do you do. Do you work around here?" The girl looked at Ray suspiciously. Why would he speak to her? "I work right upstairs here, and I've gotta get back in ten minutes or I'll be locked out. I just got this job, and my family needs me to have it. My momma, she works here, too. It's not exactly a cushy job, but you know, I just started. I sew buttons on shirtwaists. Now, my momma, she's a cutter, but she's been here a long time." Ray didn't want to ask her what a shirtwaist was, but if she sews buttons on them, he figured they were shirts of some kind. "My momma, she's a still upstairs, sneaking a cigarette from her station. But me, I wanted to come down, but I gotta go back. I don't like the job, but my Momma said that if I used my noodle, I could move up." Ray recognized a slight Italian accent. She added the word "a" in front of certain words, but she spoke English fluently. Ray wanted to learn more, and she was talkative enough. He wasn't a threat to him, and the way he was dressed, Ray figured he wouldn't be a threat to anybody else.

"You and your Momma have been here in New York for a long time?" Ray asked. The girl had no problem answering back. "A long time now. I came when I was seven, from Potenza, in 1904, you know, Basilicata". Ray didn't know, but he could make out an Italian accent, so it made sense. He figured he didn't need to question it. He wouldn't know the region, but he knew she was an Italian girl. She went on, "So now that I'm fourteen, I work, like the rest of my family." Okay, Ray, just do the math. 1904, seven years old, now fourteen. So, it was 1911. Made sense, but why was he here? No war zone, everything looked fine. "Your English is very good. What is your name?" "My name is Rosaria, but people call me Sara. We live down by Canal Street. I don't like the walk, but it's March now and it's not a too bad." Ray heard. Sara continued, "My parents, they speak Italian at home, but they understand English just a-fine, and they make a me speak English. My poppa says I am in America and I have to speak a-perfect English, so I do." Ray went on "Are there a lot of girls your age that work here?" Sara said, "I'm young but there are some others. I met a girl name Tillie Cardoza, and I like her. She's an Italian girl, too, I thought, but she told me she's a Jewish girl and lives on Essex Street, so we walk here together." Sara really didn't know about the Sephardic Jewish population, and on this one, Ray didn't either. It went right over his head.

"I actually live on Mulberry Street, and Tillie isn't far away. I got a brother. He's a real bimbo, you know. Too tough to work here." Ray was confused by the term bimbo, but her brother was tough. Okay. The year of 1911 had a language all its own.

Lower Manhattan has a storied history all its own. The original part of the city, there was a time when nobody expected the city to move any further north than Chambers Street, site of the City Hall, about two miles to the south of Washington Square Park and the adjacent Greenwich Village, once a tobacco farm and not even considered part of the city. It was then the site of New York's first penitentiary, Newgate Prison, on West 10th Street, on the Hudson. Since the prison was north of the city, residents began using the term "up the river" to describe the act of being sent to the prison, until the city grew well to the north, and then that honor switched to Sing Prison, to the north, in the town of Ossining.

Eventually, the city grew well to the north, but Greenwich Village became known as an artist's utopia, and bastion of free, progressive thought, with many political movements gathering strength there.

Sensing that the growth of Manhattan Island would continue to the north until it reached the furthest-most point, home to the Inwood neighborhood, city planners reserved a large, 2.5-mile-long escape from the city called Central Park, perhaps the best decision a major city ever made considering what Manhattan would become, although the fifteen-year project, costing over $7 million, would cost more than the purchase of Alaska, just a few years later.

In twenty years, the world's tallest building would be built way up on West 34th Street, and the city would find its destiny, from the Battery to Chelsea, from Times Square to Central Park, and from Harlem to Riverside, and Inman Park, running over thirteen miles.

But right now, Ray, in a dream, in reality, whatever he was in, was trying to make sense of the "event", and by now, he was usually able to do it, but this time, he couldn't. This young girl did not seem to be part of it. She wasn't a King or Queen, a Founding Father, a soldier. She was an underaged sweat shop worker when such things were permissible. She had to go, and he would be better served walking across the street, or across the town, to see whom else he could run into. Maybe Henry Ford was in town, maybe a Vanderbilt. Surely, somebody he could find in a library book in 1978, that Ray would, or could, have an impression upon in 1911.

"I have to go back upstairs now to the ninth floor. There is a service elevator, but we're not allowed to use it. I get one fifteen-minute break a day, and this is it. In five more minutes, they will lock the

doors, and they stay locked all day. We get checked at the end of
the day in case we've taken anything from the factory with us, but it
is still a job, and I gotta work until six o'clock this evening, so
goodbye Mister, whatever your name is. You look like somebody
with an important job to do. My job is not so important, but it is still a
job. Goodbye", and with that, she hurried through the door and was
gone.

Ray felt badly for her, but there was little he could do for her. She
would go on to live her life. Maybe, in time, she would get out of the
crowded tenements on the Lower East Side, and move to Brooklyn,
where there was some more room, or even leave the area entirely.
She would have a life of some kind, and Ray only wished he could
know what kind of life it would be, but he would not. It was time for
him to walk once more before he zoned out and found himself lying
in bed. Wasn't that always the way it happened? "The ninth floor",
he thought, and as he looked up to the confines of that floor, he
looked just above the front door to a sign that read, Asch Building,
and over a window, on one the higher floors, another sign, showing
a triangle, that read "Triangle Shirtwaist Factory". It meant nothing to
Ray except that he would have to look up in an encyclopedia when
he got home exactly what a "shirtwaist" was, besides some kind of
shirt, he supposed.

Ray walked some more, the smell of a fresh deposit of horse
manure drifted in the air. "How could people live like this?", he
thought. He walked back into the confines of Washington Square
Park, and across from the arch was a bench. He sat down on that
bench and looked onto his new watch. Well, new to him. The watch
said "11:36". I guess Sara had made it back upstairs before the
doors were locked again. How barbaric to be treated like mice in a
maze. He looked around. People were still people. A handful of
blocks to the south lay the "de Waalstraat", or Wall Street, where
George Washington took the oath of President, on the steps of
Federal Hall, and where, in 1929, the wall came tumbling down,
figuratively, with the stock market crash, but on this March day of
1911, nothing apparently was going to happen of importance, not on
Wall Street, not in Washington Square Park, and not to a young
fourteen-year old girl named Rosaria, trapped in a dead-end job.

Ray put his head back to relax, and everything went Stone.

Ray's eyes opened up, and he looked at the ceiling, a ceiling in Athens, GA. It was 7:00 AM, and he'd have to leave for school in around twenty minutes. He felt supremely dissatisfied and confused, almost cheated. He left without any breakfast and without any wisecracks from Linda. School seemed to fly by, and he was glad, because he had a job to do. Sure, there was a library at Clark Central High School, but it paled in comparison to the library system just a mile and half away at the UGA campus, with its 4.5 million volumes. The library was one of several, but the main library was at the end of the North Campus. There was the original, columned building that attached to the more modern, multi-stories building that so many students studied at each day and night. Even Ray would go there, to study, sure, but nowhere was there a better collection of history books, and this late afternoon, he had some history to explore.

He arrived and went to the reference section on the first floor and pulled out a simple encyclopedia. He began searching under "T". His fingers ran over the pages. An article on Turkey, too far. Go back a few pages. "T, R", he looked, and then he saw it, and he froze. He felt the color begin to go out of his face and felt sick to his stomach as he read the opening sentences:

"The Triangle Shirtwaist Factory fire in the Greenwich Village neighborhood of Manhattan, New York City, on March 25, 1911, was the deadliest industrial disaster in the history of the city, and one of the deadliest in U.S. history.[1] The fire caused the deaths of 146 garment workers – 123 women and girls and 23 men[2] – who died from the fire, smoke inhalation, or falling/jumping to their deaths. Most of the victims were recent Italian and Jewish immigrant women and girls aged 14 to 23;[3][4] of the victims whose ages are known, the oldest victim was 43-year-old Providenza Panno, and the youngest were 14-year-olds Kate Leone and Rosaria "Sara" Maltese."

Ray felt the tears welling up inside, and then felt them rolling down his face. He wiped them away with his shirt sleeve, and looked, self-consciously, to see if anybody was looking. They weren't. There WAS a reason or Ray to be where he was, and he did nothing. He made no difference. He didn't know. For all the history books, all the lectures from Dad, all the sitting in on "American History 101" classes, and for all the damn smugness that Ray had developed from being the "history expert" and "better, more knowledgeable in history than any students, not just at Clarke Central High School, but in UGA", and his quiet attitude that "Hell, I could teach American History 101", he failed. He was sent to save a young girl's life, but he didn't know. He didn't know the story, He failed. As he made his way to the parking lot, he felt something in his pocket. It was a pocket watch. Ray threw it in the bushes. He then went home and went back to his room, and he cried.

As of a result of the Triangle Shirtwaist Factory tragedy, New York modernized the state's labor laws, making it one of the most progressive states in terms of labor reform. New laws mandated better building access and egress, fireproofing requirements, the availability of fire extinguishers, the installation of alarm systems and automatic sprinklers, better eating and toilet facilities for workers, and limited the number of hours that women and children could work. In the years from 1911 to 1913, sixty of the sixty-four new laws recommended by a special Commission were legislated with the support of Governor William Sulzer.

As a result of the fire, the American Society of Safety Professionals was founded in New York City on October 14, 1911.

New York University Real estate speculator and philanthropist Frederick Brown later bought the Asch building and subsequently donated it to the university in 1929, when it was renamed the Brown Building, and stands today, a National Historic Landmark.

A Snub of Olympic Proportions

Ray Stone stood a few feet away from the track at the University of Georgia with his dad. Normally, the only running he enjoyed watching had to do with a quarterback handing the ball off to a running back at Sanford Stadium, but his dad liked track. Ray thought it fit his dad's personality. Discipline, preparation. Structure. For Dr. Gene Stone, perhaps. Not for his son.

It was just a track and field practice. Sprinting, jumping, a couple of javelins in the air, a couple of shot puts. Neither father nor son had the skill set to be out there, other than on the spectator side. The team would improve over the years, as would other teams on campus. The track sat on the far south campus, in the shadow of the Coliseum and football practice fields.

"C'mon, dad, let's get out of here". "Ray", said the Professor, you have no appreciation of the work it takes to be out on that track," Gene said, smiling. This wasn't a teaching moment. Just fun. They had to drive down Lumpkin Street, to a hardware store near Five Points, before heading home. "Hey, Dad, it's dollar pitcher night at 'Sons of Italy', near the hardware store," Ray said, deliberately tweaking his dad a little. "How would you know?" said Gene. Gene and Ray both knew plenty besides history. Gene let him have his fun, up to a point. "Ok, let's go", said Dr. Gene.

They went to the hardware store, but not "Sons of Italy", but that was okay. There'd be other times. Then, they headed north, crossing over Milledge Avenue and past many of the fraternity and sorority houses that served the large Greek community.

Once home, the family ate. Ray had been asking for BBQ, like they served at the Charlie Williams Pinecrest Lodge, a staple in Athens. Mom said she couldn't get it right. After all, she grew up in Menomonee, Wisconsin. If it was cheese curds, Mom could nail it, so she ordered take out from the Lodge. Wow, was it Christmas? Dad smiled because he knew it was coming. Ray didn't want to start another war between the states, but pulled pork was a heck of a lot better than walleye, mom's favorite fish growing up. Nobody could say walk away from pulled pork from Charlie Williams' Pinecrest Lodge.

It was mid April, and not much going on this Thursday. One more day of school for the week, and just a little more than a month away until summer vacation. His parents said that they didn't get out until late June, Mom in Wisconsin, dad in Chicago. Ray thought that was nuts.

Around midnight, Ray headed to bed, a little later than his parents would have liked, but his parents didn't keep a tight rein on them any more than they had to. But both he and his sister Linda were good students. Ray, a little better than his 9th grade sister, if he said so himself. The family watched part of The Tonight Show, watching Loni Anderson and Bob Hope.
It was obvious what Ray was concentrating on. Loni was one of the stars of "WKRP in Cincinnati", and had just won the first of three Golden Globes. Bob Hope was, well Bob Hope. He was always on this show, thought Ray, though Ray was more than just a little knowledgeable of Bob Hope's legendary entertainment of American troops during wartime. In fact, he was telling a story about he and Ann Margaret, in Vietnam. Couldn't Ann Margret just be there instead, and tell the story, preferably while dancing? Well, it was nice to see Loni.
Ray retreated to his bedroom, actually glad to be going to bed. It was a long day, and already just after midnight. It took all of six minutes for him to doze off.

Ray woke up, walking, as he always did when he had an event. He hated that. He felt groggy, wobbling, unsure if he would walk off a cliff or get hit by a car. If this was a dream, he had nothing to worry about. If not, he had everything to worry about.

It was a nice day, warm day. Not hot, but quite warm, considering he was wearing a suit. A suit and tie. Fairly normal, 20th century. I mean, at least it wasn't one of those horrible-looking "leisure suits" that everyone was wearing in the '70's, and already phased-out by now. There were a lot of people walking around. Most dressed quite nicely. No guns going off, no tanks. Okay, good, he wasn't in a war zone. No fires and no sirens. Things seemed festive, happy, actually. Then all of a sudden, he looked up. First, he saw a street sign, "Olympischer Platz", and then something that made him feel sick. For as long as he could see, hung up on light poles in a perfectly straight line, with military-precision, on both sides of the street, were banners. First, a banner that totally freaked him out, a large swastika inside of a circle. Each banner must have been twelve feet long, a red background with the white circle, and Stone symbol of the Third Reich. The next banner was different, the five Olympic rings, with an eagle above it, and on the front of the eagle, another swastika. The rings represented the five continents of the world, while the six colors are those that appear on all the national flags of the world at the present time. Oh my God, a horrifying first sight, but also, very easy to figure out, especially for Ray, for along with the American Revolution, World War Two, including the rise of the Third Reich, was a topic Ray knew almost as much as his Professor father about. Well, almost. This was Nazi Germany during the Olympics. It was 1936 and it was August, about the time the Olympics are always held. There were times when Ray went a long time before he could get his bearings and figure out where the heck he was.

Ray looked far down the road. It was obviously a major boulevard, and most people were walking in his direction. Men, women, families. Everybody looked so happy. This was Nazi Germany? Well, yes, for two weeks in August of 1936, Nazi Germany was a different place. At least Ray was at a point in history he understood. Ray was walking down the major thoroughfare. The 100,000-spectator Olympiastadion, the Olympic Stadium, built specifically for these games. He continued walking. Suddenly, a man wearing a crisp sport coat, white shirt, with Olympic Symbol, looked right at him, with a smile, and said "Guten Tag, darf ich Ihnen helfen, sich irgendwo zurechtzufinden?" Ray was taken off-guard. He didn't know a word of German, so he awkwardly said, "I'm sorry, I don't speak German". The man continued to smile, and answered Ray in German-accented, but perfect English. "Oh, I'm sorry. I was wishing you a good afternoon. Do you need any help finding your way?" Ray smiled back and said, "Oh, no, I'm fine. Well, yes, is the Olympic Stadium right this way?" The man nodded approvingly, and said "Yes, yes, it is". With perfect German precision, he said "From this very point, it is .8 kilometers". Ray didn't know his kilometers, but maybe that meant it was a mile. It wasn't a big deal. In fact, it was about half a mile. "Thank you very much, sir". No need to be rude to a Nazi Official, or Olympic Official, or maybe, here, it was the same thing. "My pleasure and enjoy our games". "Our games". Yes, the games of the XI was a German event. A Nazi event. There was never a time to showcase life in Nazi Germany as there would be for these two glorious weeks. For the propaganda machine to churn. Germany had won the bid for the 1916 games, but the Great War cancelled it. Of course, there WAS no "World War One", before there was a "World War Two", so it was the Great War, or the World War. Once again, Germany bid for, and won, the rights to hold the games in 1936.

These Olympics were considered "Hitler's Games" by many, but Germany was actually awarded the games in 1931, two years before "the Fuhrer" rose to the office of Chancellor. He no doubt saw the games as a great opportunity to showcase the Nazi State's beauty and strength.

Quickly, seemingly, to rise from the ruins of that Great War, and reprisals forced of Germany as the loser of that war, reprisals and reparations in the Treaty of Versailles, Germany was anxious to show the world what it can do. For some time now, it had shown, already, its racial and religious persecution of several people, but mostly, the Jews. As early as April 1933, the Nazi regime announced a boycott of Jewish tradesmen, craftsmen, lawyers and doctors, along with strong anti-Semitic propaganda that claimed the boycott was merely payback for the hostile attitude of foreign Jews. But things didn't stop there. Jews were relentlessly dragged through the mud by the government. Magazines like Der Stürmer ("the Striker") openly attacked Jews, and anti-Semitism was taught in the schools.

Anti-Semitism became the law of the land with the passage of The Nuremberg Laws , issued on the 15th of September 1935 . Nuremburg, in the southern region of Bavaria, was where, in most years, tremendous rallies were held. Jews were now officially stripped of their German citizenship. The Law for the Protection of German Blood and German Honor banned marriage and extramarital relations between Jews and Germans, the employment of German servants aged 45 and under in Jewish households and the display of German flags by Jews. Many prominent Jews, like Albert Einstein, had already left. Einstein in 1933. Others remained, certain that the German people were far too civilized to allow a crazy man like Hitler continue. The world discovered that indulging Hitler would never satiate the man's appetite for power and destruction. But, for two weeks in August 1936, any shops or signs bearing the phrase "Deutsche kaufen nicht bei Juden" (Germans don't buy from Jews) were removed. The streets were nice and clean, everybody was happy. Happy to be a German in the greatest, purest country in the world.

Not everybody was fooled, and long before the Olympics began, several counties threatened to boycott the games. Certainly, Jewish organizations lobbied for it, and even men like Judge Jeremiah Mahoney, a prominent judge, fine athlete, and President of the Amateur Athletic Union (AAU) opposed American participation in the games. The Judge was a fierce opponent of discrimination, racial or otherwise. However, a vote dispelled any notions that the U.S. team would boycott. F.D.R. chose to let the A.O.C., the American Olympic Committee, headed-up by Avery Brundage, to operate independently of the government, Brundage, like many others in the Olympic movement, initially considered moving the Games from Germany. After a brief and tightly managed inspection of German sports facilities in 1934, Brundage stated publicly that Jewish athletes were being treated fairly and that the Games should go on, as planned.

The decision to allow the United States to participate in the Berlin Olympics also persuaded other countries thinking of a boycott, to drop their complaints and attend. That did not change public opinion among many Americans, who got used to seeing newspaper articles about the persecution of Jews in everyday society in Germany. The Nuremburg Laws cemented the Jews as 2nd class citizens, by law. It was this kind of stance that allowed for violence against Jews, while the authorities looked the other way. Among the worst of these events was the "Night of Broken Glass", or Kristallnacht, or the Night of Crystal, also called the November Pogrom(s), and was a pogrom against Jews carried out by SA paramilitary forces and civilians throughout Nazi Germany on 9–10 November 1938. The German authorities looked on without intervening.

Ray was quite knowledgeable about the rise of the Third Reich, and the "Jewish Problem" which led to the "Final Solution", the extermination of the Jews throughout Europe. In 1936, all he could do was walk around and observe, and try to discover his purpose, as he always had, even if he didn't realize it until later.

Ray reached the impressive stadium after several minutes. It was round, with a section on one end, inside, where the seats gave way to an open area. It was there that the Olympic Flame burned in the breeze. Okay, so the opening ceremonies had passed, at least at some point. People were filing into the stadium. Track and Field events, or "Athletics", as it is often called, consisted of many events, so they could be on the first day or even the last, but an event seemed to be starting relatively soon. Ray had no tickets, certainly no Reichsmarks, the currency of the day, so he took a stroll around the great stadium. He heard music, saw happy people, and he saw flags. He saw lots and lots of Flags. Olympic Flags. Nazi Flags. Flags inside the stadium, which he could see peeks of now and then, and flags outside the stadium. In fact, had Ray taken a cab around town, he would have seen flags everywhere. The pageantry was impressive. The Germans were on display, and they wanted nothing to go wrong for these two weeks. That included nothing to challenge their claim of Aryan Supremacy.

Ray wasn't going to enter the stadium, so he looked to take a seat somewhere. Maybe his journey was to end soon. It often did when he sat down. Afterall, he controlled very little. He had only spoken, very briefly, with that "aide", that volunteer helping people to get around. Something was about to change.

Several feet away sat two benches, facing each other. One bench was empty. On the other sat two men, not looking much older than Ray's seventeen years, and they were wearing some kind of warmup suit, with "U.S.A." on the back of the jackets. Okay, they'll speak English. A chance to learn something. Perhaps he'd learn why he was here at all, a dream, or otherwise.

"Excuse me, is it alright if I sit here?" Ray asked the two men. They looked up. They looked extremely upset about something. One of the men shrugged his shoulders as if to say, "What do I care?". So, Ray sat. Ray had to initiate something. I mean, what did he have to lose? They were obviously Americans, apparently on the team. Maybe they were even competing soon. "Are you both on the team?" Ray asked. One of them answered, "I don't know", he said. "Hey Sam, are we on the team?" The Sam was Sam Stoller, a 21-year-old student at the University of Michigan, celebrating his birthday on this day. Perhaps "celebrating", though, was a bad choice of words". The other was Marty Glickman, still eighteen years old, for another week, so technically only a year older than Ray. "I'm Marty Glickman" said Marty, and he reached out to shake Ray's hand. "This is Sam Stoller" the Michigan Wolverine, and I'm at Syracuse" "My name's Ray, and I live in Georgia. My Dad teaches at The University of Georgia. He also went to school in Wisconsin, so I know a thing or two about Big Ten Football." "Well,", said Sam,

"Marty here plays some football. I just run, but right now we don't do much of anything." Marty spoke up, "Sam, doesn't Spec run at Georgia?" "Yeah, I think he does", said Sam. "Hey, Ray, do you know Spec Towns?" "No, sorry" said Ray. "Well, he's a hurdler at the University of Georgia". He won a Gold Medal in the 100-meter hurdles. Set a world record. There's more to life than football, you know." "Oh yeah, sure," said Ray. "You guys run, then?" "Ray, you don't know half of it", said Marty. "We're not running. We were pulled. Found out this morning during a meeting. We were both on the 4x100 relay. Busted our rear ends to get here, and just got screwed over." "Wow, I'm sorry", said Ray. "What happened?"

"Well, you want the official version, or the real version?" Marty asked. Sam looked at him as if to say, "Don't say anything you'll regret. Remember where you are". "Well,", Ray said, whatever you think you can say." Mary continued, cautiously. We were told by our coaches this morning that the Germans were holding back two stronger runners, and they were replacing us with Jesse Owens and Ralph Metcalf". "Jesse Owens?" asked Ray. Marty continued, "Oh, sure, you know Jesse. The whole world knows Jesse now". Three gold medals, probably a 4th tomorrow when he helps win the relay. "Well, why did he do that?" Ray asked. "No", Sam said, "you don't understand. It wasn't Jesse's doing. He told the coaches that he didn't want to run. Marty and I worked for this race. It isn't just speed. It's the handling of the baton as well, but it's more than that. We're Jewish. The only two on the entire track and field team. If you haven't heard, the Nazi's hate the Jews. Something is up. Something was said." "You found that out?" asked Ray. "No, we found out nothing", said Marty. "We were told what I explained to you, and when Jesse tried to help, they told him to be quiet and do what he was told." Sam took over, "Look, Jesse is a stand-up guy. We're both Ohio natives, and I've been running against him since high school. He's at Ohio State, a big rival of ours in Ann Arbor. I can tell you that except for one time, I come in second to him. But he's a good guy and deserves all the attention he's getting." Marty added, "Yeah, he's so popular now that he's signing autographs everywhere, he walks, but Hitler wouldn't even shake his hand. 'Der Fuehrer' marched right out of the stadium. He snubbed Jesse, but at least the people love him. They love him more here than they do back in America."

"So, what can you do", asked Ray? "Can you prove anything?" "I don't know" said Sam. "We were given a reason why we were pulled. We don't believe it, and never will. I'm done running, Ray. I'll never run again". Nobody said anything because given the circumstances, you really couldn't blame him, or either of them. "Well, I'm really sorry", said Ray. The two former track stars just looked at Ray. They were furious a couple of hours earlier. Now, they were in a state of shock. The anger would return, again and again. Possibly, for life. "These damn Nazi's" said Marty. "I don't know how anybody could be Jewish and live here, and I tell ya, it's gonna get worse before it gets better". Ray thought, "If only they knew, but nobody would believe it. The world couldn't believe it. Four years away from the start of another World War. Eventually, the United States would be back, Poland, France, and most every country in Europe would be overrun, and the treatment of the Jews in each of these countries would be beyond most human beings could comprehend in their wildest dreams, or in their worst nightmares. He was glad that Marty and Sam were going back to the U.S. Ray prided himself on his knowledge of history, especially World War Two, but he didn't know about Marty or Sam. There were so many good people with lives compromised, lives ruined. "I'd better go", Ray said. "I'm meeting my dad outside the stadium, soon". The men were listless, their spirits crushed. Marty just glanced ahead. Sam finally said, simply and quietly. "Okay, Ray, see ya".

Jesse Owens, along with Ralph Metcalf, another Stone athlete, helped the American Men win the 4x100 relay. The Germans had no secret weapon. They had no special runners inserted into the relay. It appeared quite obvious what was at play. It was one thing for a Stone man to win an Olympic medal. Hitler hated it, but his advisors like Joseph Goebbels, the Reich Minister of Propaganda, could not allow for Jews, whatever team they were associated with, to further upset the host country, so the understanding, or rumor, was that Nazi officials approached the U.S. Olympic team leadership, who then spoke with the track team coaches. There was some mention of the coaches showing favoritism to some of their own runners, but Glickman and Stoller, and indeed, many others through the years, felt very strongly that they understood the real reason.

Ray decided to keep walking, away from where he came, to the north. There, he saw Olympiapark Schwimmstadion Berlin, the swim stadium. That was pretty obvious, as he viewed the 50-meter pool, with eight lanes, and the smaller diving pool. It was much nicer than the pool at Stegeman Hall at Georgia. It should be. It was new. He was tired and he hoped he knew what that meant. This was not a place he wanted to be any longer. He sat down on the steps of what was the gymnastics arena. It was empty. No competition that day, apparently. He leaned back and closed his eyes.

Ray woke up in the same, usual place. There, on the other wall, was the Wisconsin and Georgia banners. Later that evening, the family had dinner. Ray didn't mention the dream, or Marty or Sam. He never did, but he did mention something else. "Hey Dad, did you know that there was a Forrest Towns that ran for Georgia in the 1930's, and he won a gold medal at the 1936 Olympics? His nickname was Specs" Gene looked puzzled, "Spec Towns? How would you know that? You don't even like track". Oh, I came across it in the library." Linda, always feeling the need to start up a sibling rivalry said, "I didn't know they served beer at the library". It wasn't bad, but Ray was ready. "Well, if you ever stepped into a library, you might know". Touché. In 1990, the University of Georgia would rename the track and field complex, the Spec Towns Track.

The festivities in Berlin may have suited the crowd. They may have believed the pageantry, they may have felt the euphoria felt by any proud nation, as they thrust their arms in unison in the arenas and stadiums, with the screams of "Zeig, Heile". Indeed, they would remain in a state of Euphoria, and believe in the cause of Aryan supremacy, through the September start of World War Two, and for some time after, as victory after victory piled up. Perhaps it wouldn't be for six years, another August, but in 1942, when the war began to turn in favor of the Allies, and against Germany. That place was called Stalingrad, and there were no banners, no pigeons flying overhead, no medal ceremonies.

Marty Glickman was both a star runner and football player at Syracuse University. Following service in the Marine Corps. during World War Two, Glickman became one of the most successful and famous sports announcers in the country, announcing for most of the major New York-area teams. He passed away in 2001 at the age of 83. Sam Stoller decided to continue running after all, and with Jesse Owens turning pro, had a stellar season, winning both the Big Ten and NCAA Championship. He actually tried his hand at singing and acting for a time, and he died on May 29, 1985, at age 69.

Jesse Owens, who said that Hitler did not snub him, but had to leave early, and waved at him, was a star in Germany. There is a "Jesse Owens Way" named after him. When he returned to the United States, he was not allowed to enter through the front doors of the Waldorf Astoria Hotel in New York, to attend an event in his honor. The President, Franklin Delano Roosevelt, did not invite him to the White House and did not contact him or send any congratulatory message. He was stripped of his amateur status because he took advantage of some endorsement offers. "You can't eat a gold medal", he was heard to say. Among the many jobs the most celebrated track star of the time had was as a gas station attendant and janitor. The pack-a-day smoker died of an aggressive form of lung cancer and died on March 31st, 1980.

In July and August 2015, the European Maccabi Games, an event that first began in Israel, and for Jewish Athletes only, was held on the site of the 1936 Olympics.

Our Gang Foibles of 1935

Gene Stone cranked up the Bell & Howell 471A Autoload Super8/8MM Film Projector, in the basement of the family's Athens, GA home. He actually had the whole crew downstairs watching, popcorn, included. This was rare. There was Carol, Lisa, and Ray. "C'mon, Dad, I don't even remember any of this!", Linda said. A lot these tapes, I'm a baby, or a year-old". "Oh, so what", Gene said. "We remember". "Look how cute you were". Ray chimed in, "Dad, not the 'Rock City' tape again!". Of course, Ray was referring to the Chattanooga attraction up on Lookout Mountain, with its rock formations, trails, and "Lover's Leap", where it is claimed that you can see seven states. There was even a Civil War Battle there. "Hey look, here's the part on top of Lover's leap", Carol said. "Oh my God, Linda looked away. I can't take those heights, even on a film!", "Well", Carol said, "you were extremely interested in jumping off". "And you didn't let her?" Ray jokingly said. "Hysterical, Ray", Linda added. Carol said, "Ray, you were four, and the drive took about three and half hours, and every twenty miles we passed a barn with the message on it that said, "See Rock City", and you keep thinking we were there." "Well, yeah", said Ray. What else could I think?"

They watched some other movies. Always trips. That's what they did. Piled the family into their 1966 Ford Country Squire station wagon, and away they went. Many times, there was a historical bent to it, as far as they could go in a station wagon. Saint Augustine, FL, Mammoth Cave, in Kentucky, Kitty Hawk, NC to Williamsburg, VA, and the biggest road trip, the 1976 "Bi-Centennial", the "Mother of all road trips", and by then, in their '77 Chevy Van.

"Hey, Dad no previews for 'Animal House'?" "Nope, no Animal House. Sorry to disappoint you". "Well, said Ray, it'll be out in two weeks". "It's supposed to be UGA", said Linda. They needed a big party school". Not Quite, said Ray, "It's not supposed to be. I read in the 'Red and 'Stone' (the local student-produced newspaper) that it was made at the University of Oregon. Anyway, I wouldn't worry if I were you. They won't be making any movies over at Watkinsville Community College" (a made-up school in a neighboring town, strictly or comedic effect). Linda would get the brotherly insult.

"Okay guys, movie night is over. I don't know about you, but I'm off to bed". Everybody pretty much agreed, and off they went. It was 11:15 when they all headed upstairs. Ray now had a TV in his room, a General Electric 19-inch. Nice. It had the standard two channel knobs, the top one for channels 2-13, and the bottom one, the UHF channel, but of course, they now had cable, so the cable box sat on top, and the channel selector stayed on channel 3 the entire time. It was a nice setup compared to years past, and it was only this year when his parents, who always said "no TV in your room!" relented. Getting excellent grades gave you some perks and even got you out of some trouble. The news was just finishing up. It was November 20, 1978, two days after the big Jim Jones Kool-Aid incident, and guest-host, Gabe Kaplan (from the show "Welcome Back, Kotter) must have felt it was safe to put a joke in his monologue. Of course, this was when cult leader Jim Jones, convinced 900 people to drink Kool-Aid laced with poison, in the country of Guyana, which Ray had heard of but virtually nobody else. It was probably the biggest "weird" news since August, when a dog told the "Son of Sam" killer, David Berkowitz, to kill several people, using a "Bulldog .44 caliber handgun". Georgia Bulldog fans weren't pleased with the association. Also on the show was actor Robert Ulrich, starring in the show "Vegas" at the time. Nobody could ever replace Johnny, even though he was often gone, so Ray shut the TV off after 30 minutes, and eventually fell asleep.

Ray woke up, standing on a staircase, literally. He looked ahead. There was a door and a building attached to it. On the door was writing. "Our Gang Cafe". So far, nothing registered. He turned around and saw a street sign that read "Washington Blvd". He saw tall palm trees. The really tall ones. Then across from that what looked almost like a 2-story house with a sign above the front doors that read. "Hal Roach Studios". Behind that were large, windowless buildings that looked like airplane hangers. They were sound stages, where movies were filmed. Ray knew the 'Hal Roach' name, but for only one reason. It was the home of the Laurel and Hardy comedies. Norvel Hardy was born and raised in Georgia, so Ray knew his story.

Ray walked up to the door and opened it. It was very crowded inside. It was 2:00 but still full. In fact, not a single table was opened. A waitress walked over and said, "It'll be a few minutes, Hon. Late lunch crowd today." Ray said "Sure, that's fine." He added

"Got a newspaper around?" The waitress said "Sure, right on the counter, help yourself". Nothing better than a paper to give you the 411 on where the hell you were in the world, and when. It wasn't always easy to get. His quick analysis, the dress, Artie Shaw playing "Interlude in B-flat" on his clarinet, he would guess 1930s. No men in uniform, and too many men, for that matter, so it wasn't '42, yet. By then, every available man between 18 and around 40, would be in uniform, or probably want to have a good excuse not to be. In fact, just a short eight miles away, over on Cahuenga Blvd in L.A., they'd open up the "Hollywood Canteen", a place just for the servicemen and women, where the stars would serve up and food and entertain. He wasn't sure what stars he might find in this place. Probably nothing like that.

Ray grabbed the paper, the Los Angeles Times. Check, November, 20th, 1937. Okay, check and check, but holy crap. Every event was shocking in its own right, but here he was, if not in 1937, then dreaming about it, and a pretty damn realistic dream it was. He really wasn't in the mood to read the paper, anyway, so he put it back down. Suddenly, a boy walked over to him. Freckle-faced kid, around ten or so. The boy pulls on Ray's sleeve, and says "Hey mister, you can sit at the booth with me if you'd like. You're probably in a hurry, waiting to get back to the set." Ray said, "Oh, well, sure, kid. I'll do that. Thanks". He followed him over to the table and sat down. Looking straight at him, the kid said "You just need to buy me my lunch. That's the deal, okay?" Ray had looked in his wallet out on the steps and noticed he had six dollars. That was rich for him. He just hoped nobody looked too closely at any serial numbers or the year on those bills, but who did that? He'd have to take his chances. "Yeah, sure, kid".

The waitress came over. "Okay, you two, what can I get ya? We've got a special today, a can of sardines with potato salad and sliced tomatoes, for 60-cents. "Uh, no thanks" said Ray. That sounded gross. May I have a minute to look-over the menu?" asked Ray. "Take all the time you want, Hon", came the reply. "Hey, Stink, did you get another mug to pay for your lunch?" The kid just smiled, then said, jokingly, "Hey Becky, don't blow your wig, huh?". Ray looked at the kid a little strangely. "Did she just call you 'Stink'"? The kid said, "Well, yeah, I'm Bobby Taylor, you know, Stinky, from Our Gang. You know? I mean, everybody knows that!" "Well, I don't watch too many 'Our Gangs'." said Ray. "What? You kiddin? Don't you go to the movies?" Ray hoped he didn't ask him to recall his favorite 1937 movie. He wasn't an old Stone-and-white movie buff. Ray played it safe, "Not really. I go to libraries, mostly. It wasn't a complete lie." "Hey listen, genius, I'm famous. I mean, I'm not Spanky or Alfalfa, but people know me". Ray considered the comment for a second. First of all, this kid was a wise-ass. "Genius?" "Ray got it. No doubt he was one spoiled kid. Okay, Spanky and Alfalfa. The Little Rascals, but everything, including the name of the restaurant, said "Our Gang". Ray turned over the menu, and any doubt he had was erased. There, right on the cover of menu, sat Spanky, Alfalfa, Darla, and a couple of other kids that Ray didn't know, but was probably supposed to know. He didn't see "Stinky" on the cover. The waitress came back. "All set, boys?" "Sure", said Ray. "I'll have the half chicken, broiled." "You know, that's 60-cents, right?. "Yeah, 60-cents is fine". "Okay, big spender, and for your, Stink? "Bobby, "Stinky" Taylor said, hey, the man here is paying, so I'll have the special". "The sardines?", thought Ray! Different times, different tastes, literally. But he DID like the prices!

"So" said, Ray, how did you get the name Stinky? Bobby answered. "Well, that's simple. I was in an episode my first year, 1932, and Mr. Gowan (Director Robert McGowan) had me pretend to eat a sandwich with limburger cheese in it. The kids all smelled it. One said 'Hey, what's that horrible smell?' So, that was my first short, and I went by Bobby, but after that, it was Stinky". Ray never heard of limburger cheese, but obviously, it smelled badly. Still, he wanted to try a little test with this wise-guy kid. "So, limburger smells bad?" "Smells, bad?", Bobby said. "Where you been, genius? You shred it wheat." Ray had no idea what that last part meant, but okay, limburger cheese smelled badly, and now this kid was called Stinky. Ray only knew a few characters from what he called "The Little Rascals", but obviously, the real, or original name, was "Our Gang". "So", said, Ray, "are you friends with Spanky and Alfalfa?" Bobby said, "Oh sure, I'm friends with Spank. He's the big cheese around here. Sure, he's a pally, but Carl, he's another story." "Who's Carl", asked Ray. "C'mon, genius. Carl Switzer. You know, Alfalfa!". Ray got a kick out of this kid, but wouldn't want to be his parent, or even be around him too long. This was a spoiled kid. Ray wondered if he knew the expression "A trip out to the woodshed", because this kid could use one. Bobby went on, "Now Carl, he's all wet, you, see?

Do you know why the café is so crowded right now?" No, said Ray, but I'm sure you do. "Well", said Bobby. "Let me give you the low-down. Carl peed on the stage lights. Stunk up the place something awful, and they had to close production for the day, so a lot of people came over here. I get along with Carl, but I keep my distance. His stepfather isn't a nice guy, but, you know, Carl's his meal ticket. He is for a lot of people. That's why he'll be right back on the set tomorrow after what he did to those lights." Stinky understood the purpose of these kids, Ray thought, the game, and that was sad. "Well", said Ray. It's funny the way he sings". Bobby looked around, as if to make sure Carl wasn't within ear distance. "Yeah, it's funny, but not to Carl. He THINKS he's good!". They both chucked, for a second. Bobby continued, "Besides, this is my last week. I'm done after this." Ray said "What do you mean, you're done?". Bobby said, "I'm eleven years old. Mr. Roach said he couldn't fit me into any more of the stories. I mean, Jackie Cooper left, Farina, Stymie, Chubby, everybody, once they get to be around this age. Spanky, he could be here forever, but the rest of us, forget it. Time to move on."

"What are you going to do?" asked Ray. "Well, I'm eleven, like I said. My mom moved us out here five years ago, when I was six. She knew about the Gang. I mean, Mr. Roach started the silent version in 1923, fourteen years ago. Can you believe that? He goes on and on, but the kids, they grow up. My Mom was crying the other day, when Mr. Roach told her that this would be the last week for me. You see, I support the family. My dad's back home in Kansas. He hurt his back during the War, in Cantigny, and then after the market crashed, it was really hard for him to find anything, and my mom just took me out here. I haven't seen my Dad for about four months now. I get $110 per week now. It has to pay for everything. My mother says we'll stay and see if I can find another job, but I'd just like to go back to Kansas. "Back to Dorothy and Toto, huh?", Ray's attempt at being cute. "What in the world are you talking about?" Bobby said. Ray laughed and thought, "Oh, well, I guess it's a little early for the Wizard of Oz reference. That would come in 1939, the greatest year in cinema. Ray thought of adding "I guess your career is 'Gone with the Wind', another 1939 reference, but that would only produce another strange look, and eventually, with this kid, a sarcastic remark. He was clearly used to getting his way, even if he didn't get the same time on the screen as Alfalfa and Spanky. Ray knew the history, the abandonment, the disillusionment from going from meal-ticket and beloved star, or even semi-star, like Stinky, to a nobody, an eleven-year-old "has been". It didn't seem right, even for this eleven-year-old kid going on twenty. He said "Oh, never mind". Bobby went on, "If I can't get anything, I'll have to go home." Ray asked, "Well, I hope you get some of that money. It's yours." Bobby said "Yeah, I get a Lincoln once a week". Ray knew he meant a five-dollar bill. "But where's the rest of it?" Bobby said, "I don't know. My Mom said she'd be taking care of it." Except his parents weren't taking care of it. They were spending it.

The best-known example of child-star financial mismanagement, or outright theft, was in the case of Jackie Coogan, so much so that a law was passed in 1939, known as the Coogan Bill, specifying that at least 15% of a child actor's income be put in a trust. Years earlier, in the 1920s, Jackie Coogan gained fame as a wonderful child actor, starring in movies with Charlie Chaplin. At first, his father carefully and conservatively managed his money, but his father died, just two years earlier, in 1935, in a car accident that Jackie was also involved in, and Jackie's best friend was also killed in. His mother and stepfather later spent nearly all of his money, and Coogan sued them.

So, Bobby Taylor was likely done as a child actor, at the advanced age of eleven, but who knows? Ray and Bobby both knew that day that he was done with the Our Gang Series.

"Well, anyway, I got to have a lot of fun, and see some stars from time to time. Hey, speaking of stars, look who just walked in." Ray couldn't believe it, but it was Stan Laurel, Oliver "Babe" Hardy, and Hal Roach. Laurel and Hardy were not in their trademark Stone suits, just with some papers that Stan Laurel, the British comedian, was holding. They sat down and began having a small meeting of some kind. Ray really wanted to go meet them, especially Oliver Hardy, but was having a hard time mustering up the courage. Bobby said, "I wouldn't bother them if I was you". Ray left the table to use the rest room, then began walking back. "C'mon Ray", he thought. Think about this. If this is a dream, just do what you want. There's nothing to lose. So, Ray passed their table, turned around, and quickly said to Oliver Hardy, "Excuse me, but didn't we meet at the Turner-Butler Hotel in Madison (Georgia)? Oliver Hardy, "Babe" to his friends, stopped, and said, "excuse me?" Ray started to repeat the question, and Oliver said "No, I heard you. I haven't heard that name in years, and I didn't expect to hear it today. Who are you?". Ray said, "Oh, I'm just a kid from Athens, Georgia that liked to hitch a ride down to Madison once in a while." Ollie smiled and said, "You don't say". Well, young man, it's really great to meet somebody from Georgia. You know, I miss the place." Ray explained how he was in California for a little holiday and going back the next day. Babe Hardy introduced him to his longtime partner, and to Hal Roach, and Oliver said, "You know, son, I needed to meet you today. It's been one of those days.". He shook everybody's hands. Ollie and Stan then paid Ray their highest compliment. Ollie played with his tie, his trademark gesture, and Stand rubbed the top of his head and put on his signature face. It was classic. "Thanks for your time, all three of you", and Ray went back to his table and paid the bill. The entire bill came to around $2.00, and Ray doubled it, and the waitress was very happy about that.

Ray wished Bobby good luck. "You're a smart kid. You're be okay, Stink". Bobby smiled and said, "Okay, flatfoot, and thanks for the grub". Ray had a way with people because Bobby didn't usually thank people for anything. They both smiled. Bobby wasn't really as tough as he thought he was. He just had to grow up fast, and Ray hoped that he could somehow put his mild stardom in perspective, but Ray was worried about him. It was a good while it lasted. Time to move on. Nobody owes this kid anything. Ray hoped he would remember that.

He walked outside to the warm Culver City weather and thought about how difficult life was for people of this time. The situation was better in '37 than it had been a little earlier, with the depression on since '29. Hollywood helped a lot of people forget their troubles. Movies, and comedy shorts like Harold Lloyd, Laurel & Hardy, and the Our Gang Series, all filmed at the Roach studios across the street, helped people forget their problems.

There was to be, sadly, a very long road of discarded childhood actors that couldn't find their way in the real world. Carl Switzer would struggle to find work after his Our Gang days and would be shot to death after threatening an acquaintance in their home. Others would simply die young, like Chubby Chaney, Bobby "Wheezer" Hutchins, Matthew "Stymie" Beard, and Darla Hood. Spanky's sidekick in the series, little Scottie Beckett, went on to several promising roles, but his life spiraled downward, and he died, apparently after a beating, at the age of 38. Even George "Spanky" McFarland would die in his 60s, his life cut short by health issues. All the many problems of the Our Gang stars have caused many to consider the series cursed.

But the challenge of moving on from childhood stardom is hardly reserved for this Hal Roach Classic. Kids from the world of movies, TV and music have seen tragic results from their stardom at any early age. Many have died from drug overdoses, committed robbery, or gotten themselves into trouble in a number of ways.

As for Bobby "Stinky" Taylor, he went back home to Kansas after four months of trying to get more work in the entertainment field. He was enrolled in public school. That new environment for a kid used to the highlife did not work out well. Bullied, and with the inability to be treated like a star, he was moved around to several schools, and later on, moved from menial job to menial job. He began to drink and died at the age of 41 from cirrhosis of the liver.

Oddly enough, Hal Roach outlived most all of his childhood stars, living to the ripe old age of 100, and dying in 1992. He brought the world so many laughs through his stars.

As for Ray, he hit the jackpot, because as he roamed around Washington Blvd, Oliver Hardy saw him and brought him into the studio and gave him a tour of the offices, the sound stages, wardrobe, and more. He dozed off as he sat in one of the offices waiting to meet a makeup person.

Ray woke up in bed as he usually does and went off to school. He thought about Stinky and everybody else that he met, even the waitress who called him "Hon". He liked it.

Ray's dad, the calm, cool, and collected Dr. Eugene Stone, once told Ray that "slow and steady wins the race". Ray realized on this latest adventure that when you've given riches or attention, or both, before you can handle it, before you can sustain it, and then it's suddenly taken away from you, and at such a young age, you're not prepared to start over. These young kids, cute and adored for but a moment, are suddenly told that they're no longer cute, no longer "special", the damage to their psyche is too strong to overcome.

At dinner that night, the subject of the family movies came up again. "You know", Dr. Gene said, "it was a lot of fun watching you two as babies and toddlers. We've got some other movies we should watch soon". "That's fine Dad", but I'm glad I was just able to move on from my moviemaking stardom" joked Ray. "I'm glad you and Mom helped me keep my feet on the ground. I was a star, but you helped me move on." There was a pause, as if to say, "What the hell are you talking about?". Linda, in her special, sisterly way, broke the ice by blurting out, "In your dreams, Ray".

During the day, Ray ran over to the college library, and tried to see what he could learn about Our Gang, and Bobby "Stinky" Taylor. He found articles on the Rascals, on Hal Roach, but nothing on Stinky Taylor. It wasn't a later time, when you could "Google" anything and everything, down to the last assistant, the last credit, in a production. Instead, he found several vague articles and references, but nothing on Bobby. He didn't know that by this time, Bobby was dead from his drinking problem, in 1967.

That night, he tuned into a new show that premiered that month, November, 1978, called "Different Strokes". It featured two young Stone Boys adopted by a wealthy man. One was a little kid named Gary Coleman, funny, smart, (smart alec, to be precise), beyond his years. He reminded Ray of Stink in so many ways. He knew that their days in the limelight would probably be short as well, and hoped that they fared better than the "Gang" back in Culver City.

Directions

"Pull out the map".

Oh my God. If that wasn't the Stone family official slogan, it should have been. It was used, interchangeably, with "pull out the atlas". Of course, there were acceptable variations, such as "just look at the darned map" and "Linda, would you please learn how to use a map?" Ray liked that one. Ah, the enjoyment of bashing your loving sister! In reality, Linda was a math person. She liked to say that Ray and their dad were "so much alike", but aside from their love of history, it wasn't at all true. Linda shared dad's personality of precision, of everything being Stone and white. Being practical. Right and wrong. For all of Ray's teasing of his little sister, her math skills were off the chart. Mom majored in math at Wisconsin, and Linda, going into the 10th grade, was on a college level. Actually, past college. The parents sent her off to a tutor for private lessons in calculus and trig, and yet, she couldn't read a map. Truth was, she didn't WANT to know. Linda and her dad were the kind of people that could put together a grill without the instructions, but of course, always used them. Dad would find a better way to have written the instructions. Ray, on the other hand, got it wrong three times before he eventually figured it out. If the instructions said, "average time to assemble, 30 minutes", Dad and Linda would do it in fifteen minutes, and Ray, two hours. For real.

Ray felt that what he lacked in common sense he made up for in "people skills". People opened up to him. He wasn't sure why. He liked to talk as much as he liked to listen, but he was definitely a "right- brained person", less methodical, less mathematical. Ray was a dreamer, a thinker, but not analytically speaking. Yup, Linda was like Dad. Only, Ray wasn't going to pay her the compliment. Maybe one day. Doing that would upset the sibling rivalry, and Ray would never hear the end of it. Nobody knew that world leaders and people from different periods in time told Ray some of their most private feelings, and NOBODY could know that. They were dreams. Having any other theory wouldn't be at all practical, but then again, Ray wasn't wired to be practical.

Of course, maps were central to the Stone family because of their constant road trips, always with some kind of "historical purpose". A trip purely for the fun of it would disturb his dad's sensibilities. "Hey Dad, can we just go to Orlando and see Mickey and his friends, then the beach?" asked Linda. "You know, have some fun? Get out of the classroom?" "C'mon" said Dr. Gene. "Don't you want to learn something?" asked her Dad. "I've learned plenty, Dad" answered Linda. "You've learned, nothing" wisecracked Ray. "YOU'VE LEARNED NOTHING", answered Linda, in her trademarked "dumb male" accent she reserved for these special times. "That's it?" asked Linda, with a smirk. Ray just smiled, because at the moment, yes, that was it.

Nobody went through a Rand McNally Atlas faster than the Stone Family. It wasn't long before pages were marked, highlighted, torn, with a flyer inserted here and there, or a restaurant menu. Just when it was full of all of the great little notes, here came the new Atlas, a new one each year. Their 1979 edition was a "55th Annual Edition" showing trees with their fall colors. Some people collected atlases like others collected TV Guides, like Ray once did, but for Dr. Gene, there was nothing practical about that. "Why do you hold onto that junk", asked his Dad. "C'mon, dad!" Ray would tease his dad. I've got all the 1971 covers. Ray was ten at that time. "Look, the Mod Squad, the Brady Bunch.....Mason Reece! That kid's going places!" Even Dr. Gene laughed at that one. "Okay, Ray, keep your worthless TV Guides". "It's history, Dad!" joked Ray. That was true, but everything was history.

Dad and Ray did share a love of maps. Dr. Gene for the preciseness of it, the functionality, the practicality. He liked seeing that the newest map of Athens had listed the new Georgia Square Mall out on the Atlanta Highway. The map makers, the cartographers at Rand McNally picked up on that. How did they gather up all new malls, buildings, everywhere? Gene marveled at it all. No wonder there had to be a new edition every year. The highways and road attractions changed, so the maps had to change.

Ray loved the beauty of maps, the history, the romance of it. The romance? Well, sure, why not? While maps and atlases can get you to Asbury Park, NJ via the Garden State Parkway, at exit 102, or to "South of the Border" in Dillon, SC, at exit, 1, it has a wonderful, amazing history to it that goes back thousands of years.

Crude forms of map making began some 14,500 years ago, where dots were discovered in caves, mapping out stars in the sky. Other cave paintings mapped out features in the area, such as mountains and rivers. Clay tablets in ancient Babylonia around 7,000 BC contained maps. Phoenician sailors made great inroads in mapmaking, and by circumventing Africa, some experts predicted that by 600 B.C., the Phoenicians knew that the Earth was not flat, but spherical. Anaximander was the first ancient Greek to draw a map of the known world. It is for this reason that he is considered by many to be the first mapmaker. After that, many map makers established themselves throughout the known world, from the middle east, to portions of Europe, including the Roman Empire, to significant map making in China.

Over the years, cartography has seen tremendous developments. It has aided in travel, skills honed by great explorers leading all the way up to modern time when electronics, computers, and digital breakthroughs increased the accuracy of topography and maps. Maps have been written on cave walls, clay tablets, and then, through time, on a wide variety of materials, papers, and surfaces. Maps have been made for navigation, wartime planning, commerce, and more. People have depended on maps for exploration, for family travel, to draw-up battle plans, for trucks to route the best, most economical means of getting from point "A" to point "B". Maps have even been made to determine where to land space vehicles on the moon and Mars. There will never be an end to maps, only a continuing evolution as to how they are made, produced, and delivered.

Map making, or cartography, is a highly developed skillset, a business, a trade, and an art form. It's an entity that both Ray and his Dad, Dr. Gene, could agree on is amazing, but for different reasons. Ray's dad liked the precision. He liked to look for mistakes just as he might at reviewing a student's test. "Ahh, they missed the new courthouse building that went up last year". For Ray, it was art. He loved wall maps and globes. As a younger kid, he was often seen spinning a globe and then putting his finger down somewhere, making the globe stop. Where did he land? Oops, in the ocean, of course, as water comprised about 70% of the Earth's surface. Another spin. Okay, Greece. What could he learn about Greece, the "cradle of Democracy" that he didn't already know? This was Ray. Greece is too easy. They've given the world too much. Let's try to find some obscure place. Mali? Okay, let's hit the encyclopedia and become the neighborhood expert on Mali. That was Ray's thinking. Dr. Gene saw maps as an opportunity to critique. That's what professors did, right? Okay, and teach, for in every map, there was story. After all, maps are representations of places. Real places and real people. Places and people with a history. Everything has a history, doesn't it? People, places, even maps. It all comes down to history. Well, if your name is Stone.

Since the mid-1990s, the use of computers in map making has helped to store, sort, and arrange data for mapping in order to create map projections. But in 1978, paper maps were an essential part of vacation planning, of navigating around town or far away, for studying, and for dreaming.

The Stone family had traveled to the Savannah, GA area from Athens, GA, over 300 miles and nearly four hours by car. Dr. Gene had a conference at Armstrong State College in Savannah, and there was some time to kill after the meeting. While he spoke, the rest of the family took a trip over to River Street, then of course, to a historical landmark, Fort Pulaski, built after the War of 1812, with its 11-foot walls, considered impenetrable.

Following that visit, it was time for the Stone family to head home. Dr. Gene would do all the driving. Along the way, Ray, in the back seat, began to doze off and begin another adventure.

Ray awoke to a hell on Earth. The first thing he noticed was the smell. It was a terrible, burning smell, and smoke everywhere. He began to cough. He noticed that he was standing on a sandy beach. In one direction was either an ocean or a very large lake. He could not see the other side. He was joined by perhaps hundreds of people. He couldn't recognize the clothing as the people were a mess. He heard sirens, screams, and the thick smoke was everywhere. In the other direction, the sky was orange. He could see flames to the west, perhaps just a mile away.

Ray didn't know where he was. It was chaos. There was a huge fire, a city on one side and a great body of water on the other. People in the water. People coughing, screaming, crying. He couldn't make out a skyline. What skyline, anyway? If there was a skyline, soon, there wouldn't be. There would be nothing, not from where he could see. The beach became more and crowded. Where would he go? The air was thick with smoke, and it was hard to breathe.

Suddenly, several men walked quickly onto the sand. They were carrying two large machines of some kind that looked very heavy. They were laboring, breathing hard. The addition of all the smoke made things much worse. They were wearing heavy-looking clothing. It must have been one hundred years earlier. He wasn't sure and nobody was going to talk to him about today's date. It wasn't a day for this. It was a day about survival, and Ray wanted to survive. One day he might not ever leave the place he suddenly showed up in.

A man in the group looked at Ray. "Sir, please, help us if you can". Ray answered, "What can I do?". The man said. "We couldn't save the building or anything else, but we've got to try and save these printing presses. We have no business without them. Please, take this shovel and dig." Ray took the shovel and started digging. The machines, printing presses, were wrapped up in cloth, or perhaps blankets, so he couldn't really see much of them. Ray began to shovel, but it wasn't easy. It was sand. As he dug, some of the sand fell back in. There weren't really any waves to fill in the hole that was beginning to form, slowly. Ray suspected this was a lake, and in every direction along that side of the city, there was water. A large city and a large lake. Was it Lake Michigan? Was this the Great Chicago Fire? When was that? The 1800s, but when? Dr. Gene would not be happy, but Ray didn't know that date, and right now, why the hell would that even matter? Men were asking him to dig a hole in the sand to save a couple of printing presses, when he was having a hard enough time just breathing on his own. He needed to get away from this smoke, which meant getting away from this fire. What fire was this? It wasn't the time to ask questions. Ray continued to dig. Even in sand, you can dig, especially without waves, so with several men digging, laboring, coughing, and yes, some people along the shore throwing up, the hole got bigger. Two men argued if the hole was large enough. "No, keep digging! It won't fit yet. No, deeper, it must be covered all the way. Keep going." Eventually, the hole was pretty darned big and very clumsily, the printing presses were slid, pushed, toppled over, set back up again, and then lowered into the hole. Covering it up was easier than digging. It was simply a matter of using all the sand left in piles right next to them. Ray had one of three shovels. After all, how many shovels do you keep in a printing office? So, Ray kept shoveling pile after pile on top of the printing presses. Finally, it was done.

One of the men turned to Ray and spoke. "Thank you, young man. Your kindness is most appreciated." He had an Irish accent, or was it a Scottish accent? Ray couldn't tell although it really wasn't that hard. It simply wasn't the time for a lesson in linguistics or European accents. Ray did a lot to help and he wanted to know a little more. In this case, he felt he deserved something. A little help. "Excuse, but who are you gentlemen?" Ray thought, "Be nice, this isn't 1978, so 'who the hell are you' probably would fly."

"I'm Andrew McNally" came the reply. The man was young. Perhaps in his 30s. "This is my business partner, William Rand". We run a printing business here in Chicago. We print railroad tickets, schedules, and some other documents. "Mr. Rand and Mr. McNally", thought Ray. "You've got to be kidding me", thought Ray.

It was anything but the right moment for Ray to have his fun with his knowledge, stemming from living in 1978 and not whatever date he was in, but certainly, in the 1800s sometime, so he simply said "Oh, yes, the Rand McNally company", came the reply. Given this tremendous fire, the desperation, and fact that this young man was among them, in the city of Chicago, Mr. McNally simply said the obvious "Yes". After all, their business began in 1858, more or less, and they officially started the company ten years later. Ray wouldn't know those kinds of dates. He wasn't studying for one of his dad's tests. He did, however, know one thing. This was the great Chicago fire. It could be nothing else. He heard it was started by a cow kicking over a lantern on the O'Leary farm. That was the legend. Ray didn't know what was true or not. But wait, did Ray just save the map-making company of Rand McNally? Sure, they saved themselves before Ray, but Ray did help. If only he could tell his Dad. There were other maps, other companies. Of course, there was, but there was only one Rand McNally. Ray promised himself to be careful in how he spoke to people. After all, it might not even be a dream. He never did really know. This putrid smoke clogging up his lungs, the people dying on the ground, the chaos, the craziness, it was no time to have fun guessing what Mr. Rand and Mr. McNally were up to at this moment in time, except trying to survive, like everybody else.

"Mr. McNally, I am walking along the shore, and trying to get away from this", said Ray. "Certainly, my boy, and thank you for helping us". "Will you be okay, Ray asked". "Well, I believe so. We'll see the condition of this fire by dawn and then dig these machines back up and see if we can put them back to work." That's exactly what they did, three days later.

The "Great Chicago Fire" took place during October 8-10, 1871. It killed over 300 people and destroyed about three square miles. Approximately 100,000 people were left homeless. The weather had been very dry, and the fire was suspected of starting on the O'Leary property, though the tale of the cow and the lantern is up for debate. The fire was so strong that it jumped over the Chicago River and began burning portions of the central business district, to the north of the river. At one point, the river disrupted the ability of the city to even pump water, and the fire, aided in part by some rain, eventually burned-out.

Most of the city's structures were made of wood, and "fire whirls" a tornado-like effect of hot and cool winds merging, spun debris high into the air, allowing it to spread quickly.

Chicago is known as a tough, resilient town, and lumber began to appear in the city for the purposes of rebuilding before the last glowing building was cool. Donations poured in from around the world. The city of London, England even started a program to help build and fill a library with books. New fire codes were written to help prevent fires like this in the future, and Chicago became a great city once again.

Rumors spread quickly about the O'Leary's, including the cow and the lantern. Anti-Catholic and anti-Irish sentiments were running high in the country, and in Chicago, during that time. The O'Leary's said that they were already in bed. In any event, the rumor persisted, and the city was rebuilt.

Ray walked to the north, his feet touching the waters of Lake Michigan. He wasn't alone. He eventually walked two or three miles, late into the night. He came to rest at a point north of downtown, about a mile north of what is today, Lincoln Park, with its famous zoo already incorporated, in 1868. Fortunately, Ray did not encounter the zoo's bear, known to escape and roam the park at night, because he did not make Lincoln Park his home until 1874, in another three years.

Ray had never been more exhausted in his life. He felt what was to become some blisters on his hands, from frantically shoveling sand. He was wet from some soft drizzling that had become, sweaty, dirty, and smelled of smoke. But he was alive. He reached a soft embankment of sand, with some grass, now far from the fire, and although he could still smell smoke, the winds, at least for the moment, had generously decided to shift to the west, bringing in some fresh air from over the lake. Ray sat down on the small dune, like so many others. Exhausted. He lay there, wondering about the people who had to rebuild their lives, about the great city Chicago would yet become, once again. This time, eventually, a city of steel and glass, a city of great commerce, of map-making, of wonderful food, and yes, even wonderful sports fans, win or lose. Ray dozed off.

Ray woke in his usual place, and he suspected it was a Sunday, and he was right. The family had returned late, the night before, from their Savannah trip. There really wasn't anything to do that day. Ray went downtown and hung around and came back in the afternoon.

Later that night, he watched some TV, and pulled out his collection of 1971 TV Guides. January 9th, Andy Griffith, February 13th, Goldie Hawn, June 12th, Lucy (only one name is necessary), November 12th, The Cast from "All in the Family", and December 25th, A Christmas Tree. Wait! There's a missing week? Where is December 18th? LISA!! Ray barged into her room. "Lisa, where the hell is my TV Guide from December 18th, 1971? It's the only year where I have every copy!" "How should I know", said Lisa. "Maybe I was looking at it. Go look in my closet. Ray ran into the closet and sifted around. Finally, he found it. It was the Partridge Family Cover, and Lisa was seven in 1971, with a giant crush on David Cassidy. Lisa looked to see what TV guide she had taken and put in the closet, probably months earlier, and she laughed. "Do NOT take my TV Guides again…. ever", said an annoyed Ray. Lisa walked out of her room, singing a little tune, aimed very sarcastically at Ray "I think I love you, so what are you so afraid of." Ray looked with admiration at his missing TV Guide, happy that his entire 1971 set was still intact, and looking at some painful blisters on his hands.

With or without Ray's assistance, Rand McNally started printing maps, and became synonymous with the art and the technology, of map-making. They assisted millions for work and for play, and as the times have changed so has the company. While many people look onto digital devices like smart phones, to get their directions, many still like to hold a paper map in their hands, or an atlas, or to adorn their walls, in offices, bedrooms, and classrooms. Truckers need assistance in navigating highways. Rand McNally still makes maps, in different ways, different content, and several generations of McNally's steered Rand McNally, until they gave up the reigns of the company to other groups. The company has survived through many challenges, like other great companies, though perhaps none as so great as the night of the Great Chicago Fire.

As for the O'Leary cow, it took 126 years, but the Chicago Committee on Police and Fire voted
to exonerate Catherine O'Leary and her infamous cow on October 28, 1997:

"Be it resolved that we, the Mayor and members of the Chicago City Council assembled this 28th day of October 1997, do hereby forever exonerate Mrs. O'Leary and her cow from all blame in regard to the Great Chicago Fire of 1871."

GIANT LEAP

Ray Stone walked out along a quiet pier, just as the faintest sign of daybreak was appearing over the eastern horizon. Behind him, the coast of Florida and planet Earth, above him, the moon, and stars. He had company that early morning, a quiet, introspective man, looking for a moment's solace from a world of television cameras and flashbulbs, and the pressures of becoming the first man to ever set foot on the moon.

At first, Ray, wasn't even sure he would take a walk down that pier. He had stood in a parking lot, the town in back of him, and the ocean in front. He looked behind him and saw a store that said, "Cocoa Beach Hallmark". Well, that helped. Too early to buy a greeting card, or to do anything else. The evening was haunting. Out ahead, to the east, at the far reaches of the evening sky, he saw the tiniest glimpse of orange and yellow. Ever so faint. In time, there will be daybreak, when the diffused light is replaced by the rim of the sun breaking the horizon.

As Ray got closer to the end of the pier, he saw a man standing there, silent, watching what would be the sunrise. He either didn't notice Ray or didn't want to notice him. Ray wanted to stay out of his way. In the dark like this, over several feet of water, of waves, what would this man think of Ray, and what would Ray think of him. He reached the end but sat down at the other end, a safe-enough distance away.

After a moment, the man, wanting to judge for himself that he could keep his back to Ray, turned his head ever so slightly, not in a threatening way. Ray could see him and was immediately in a state of shock. He stood open-eyed as the Commander of Apollo 11, Neil Armstrong looked at Ray, saw a young boy, and smiled slightly. "Good Morning" came the voice. Ray was speechless. After an awkward three seconds, Ray stuttered out, "Good morning, sir". He then felt the need to add "I'm sorry if I'm disturbing you. I'll stay out of your way, sir". The Commander smiled a little more broadly, out of the appreciation for Ray's courtesy, and said, "No problem. I'm sure you enjoy a good sunrise, too". Ray shut his mouth while Commander Armstrong turned back around. The sun had still not broken the sky's surface, but would, soon. Ray did not wish to bother this man, and truth be told, was too shocked to do so.

Ray had met great men before, whether in a dream or not, and it always felt extremely real to him. Important men. Troubled men. Men with many things on their minds, men responsible for great moments in history. Yet, Ray had never come face to face with a man who would be walking on the surface of the Moon, because it simply hadn't happened before. He didn't know the date, but there was just something in his gut that told him this great event hadn't happened yet but was fast-approaching. Ray would be staring out in the ocean, and up to heavens, too, if he were in this man's position. This was a man seeking solace, and he wasn't about to bother him. Maybe he should walk back to the mainland, leaving Mr. Armstrong alone with his thoughts, but he was invited to stay, more or less, so he also got lost in his own thoughts for a few minutes.

What goes through the mind of a man about to change history, about the leave the safety of Earth's gravity, to accomplish what mankind has dreamed about since the beginning of time? Man's great quest to travel beyond his surroundings, to discover new places, across a plain, or an ocean, or now, across an expanse of space that never ends, and now he is about to go to a place only dreamed about by other great men, other great explorers.

On September 12, 1962, President John F. Kennedy threw down the Moon gauntlet, in a speech given at Houston's Rice University:

"We choose to go to the Moon...We choose to go to the Moon in this decade and do the other things, not because they are easy, but because they are hard; because that goal will serve to organize and measure the best of our energies and skills, because that challenge is one that we are willing to accept, one we are unwilling to postpone, and one we intend to win, and the others, too."

Win? Win against whom? Why, the Soviets, of course. On October 4, 1957, the Soviets launched Sputnik I, the world's first artificial satellite, which circled the Earth every 96 minutes, travelling at 18,000 miles per hour. Its radio signals could be picked up by even amateur radio operators, and it ushered in a new age, the space race. Already bitter adversaries, Americans did not like the idea of our political and ideological enemy being scientifically advanced over the USA.

Perhaps the real space race started not with the launch of Sputnik, but with the contest between members of Operation Paperclip and

Operation Osoaviakhim. What in the world was that? Well, that was the American and Soviet names, respectively, for the efforts to find and resettle thousands of German rocket scientists, following the surrender of the Nazis, in 1945. It was men like this, men like Werner Von Braun and his V-2 rocket team, that set the wheels in motion, that was largely the reason a man like Neil Armstrong even sat on this pier, just 4.8 miles from Cape Canaveral.

The names of scientists were discovered on the "Osenberg List" named after a Nazi official who assembled the list of German scientists, most of them on the Eastern Front, forced to perform menial tasks, including KP duty. It was only when the Germans' failed attempt to conquer the USSR, Operation Barbarossa, that the Nazis wanted scientists on the home front, to prepare rocketry that might protect their homeland against a protracted war against the Soviet Union. This list was subsequently discovered and landed in the hands of British, and then, American intelligence. So, when the war ended, and it was known that the Allies would now have a new nemesis, the Soviets, the race was on to find the best and brightest former Nazi rocket scientists.

The most celebrated of the German scientists, at least of those who made their way to America, was Werner Von Braun, architect of the mighty Saturn V rocket that would propel Armstrong, Collins, and Aldrin to the Moon, with an 8-million-pound thrust. Von Braun, and many of his fellow scientists would eventually settle in Huntsville, Alabama, and what would be called the Marshall Flight Center. Six of the 15 built Saturn V rockets, and its three stages, would help in bringing astronauts to the surface of the moon.

Space travel was fraught with risk and danger, and it was only two and half years, on January 27, 1967, when the three astronauts of the first Apollo Mission was killed in a pre-launch fire on the Cape Canaveral launchpad. One of the victims was Gus Grissom, a famous member of the "Mercury Seven", the first group of Astronauts to fly in space, and, like Armstrong, a fellow Purdue Boilermaker. That group consisted of Alan Shepard, Gus Grissom, Gordon Cooper; Wally Schirra, Deke Slayton, John Glenn, and Scott Carpenter. Greater heroes America never had, but in Armstrong, America would have one more.
Some of the sun was peeking over the horizon, its rays clearly visible. Within just a couple of minutes now, the top of the sun would be visible. Soon, in a matter of a day or two, the astronauts of Apollo

11 would see the Earth from the vantage point of space, a view only a few have ever been so fortunate to see outside of a photo. The view of the Earth from space has been called the "Overview Effect", where perceptions and feelings of our world change. Later, an astronaut on Apollo 14, Edgar Mitchell, would summarize it this way:

> *"You develop an instant global consciousness, a people orientation, an intense dissatisfaction with the state of the world, and a compulsion to do something about it. From out there on the moon, international politics look so petty. You want to grab a politician by the scruff of the neck and drag him a quarter of a million miles out and say, 'Look at that, you son of a bitch.'*

What would Commander Armstrong feel, and the other astronauts? What was he thinking now? Oh, how Ray would like to speak with him! Tell him everything would be okay. There would be no fire, only history made. The right history. Glorious history. But he couldn't. This was a man that must stay undisturbed, for the world would shortly be watching his every move. All of them, but make no mistake, that first step seen by hundreds of millions around the world. People in astonishment.

What was Neil Armstrong thinking? Ray continued to wonder. What would any man think looking up to the heavens? This was a different man. A special man in so many ways, but was he really special?

He might be thinking over all the many steps and procedures he would be responsible for. Would he do what was being asked of him? All the hundreds of thousands of people who have toiled to make this mission a reality. What might go wrong? Would he even return? So many questions.

What does a man do for an encore that has done what no man before him has done? All the years of flying, of preparation. Of watching helplessly while three brave men perish in a fire, alone, high up in a tiny capsule. Unable to open the hatch before they are asphyxiated. What nightmares, along with the dreams has this man experienced. This man a mere ten feet away, watching the sun rise? So many questions.

Yes, what WOULD this man do for an encore? What could possibly be more important, or satisfying, or brave, than what he was about to do within days? Could he cope with the aftermath? The game? The letdown? Will walking across the street for a cup of coffee be the same after you've walked across the surface of the Moon? Ray couldn't know, but this man at the pier, he'll find out.

What was out there? The Moon right now. That was there. One step at a time. Yes, one small step. But what was beyond that? Ray learned that light travelled at 186,000 miles per second. That was a speed he couldn't comprehend at all. Could anybody? Yet, he also read that stars he could see with his own eyes, some still visible at this very moment, before the sun's rays blocked it out, were thousands, maybe millions of light years always. Not miles. Years. Light years. Billions of miles, or more. Light he could see right now, stars, were first cast out into space hundreds or thousands of years ago, and Ray was just now seeing that light. Perhaps that star he can see is no longer even there. It was simply too much to take in. Ray remembered a friend making an explosion sound and pointing to his head, to describe a head exploding when confronted with information or questions that the brain simply couldn't deal with. This was one of those moments. Ray followed history, like his dad. This was beyond history. History was in the past, recorded. Space was another matter. Theories existed, but what was real? What was out there? So many questions.

Was Commander Armstrong thinking beyond the mission? Beyond the millions from Earth watching, was anyone else? Scientists theorized that billions of stars were in the universe. How many had inhabitable planets? What were they like? Did any have intelligence far beyond our own? Do they know we're here? Do we know they exist? Did an alien spaceship really land near Roswell, NM? What about all the UFO sightings, and encounters? Was everybody crazy? So many questions.

Finally, if Commander Armstrong didn't think it, then Ray did.

Did we matter?

A spec in the universe. Maybe there were millions of Earths. If the Earth didn't matter, why would one person? Why would a random act of kindness matter in the grand scheme of things? Does life matter, or death. Does it matter to laugh, or cry, or to worry about anything? Does love matter? Yes, so many questions, with none, seemingly, to be answered on this pier during this July dawn of 1969, or 1978, for that matter.

It was no easy feat to get across those 238,000 miles, the distance from Earth to the Moon.

Apollo 11 would lift off from Cape Canaveral on July 16th, 1969, at 9:32 AM, with over 650 million people glued to television sets around the world. The Saturn-V rocket, at 6.5 million pounds, would provide the massive thrust needed to escape the Earth's gravity. This rocket's first massive stage would separate at 42 miles, then the other two would ignite in turn, and then separate, dropping into the Atlantic Ocean. The first two stages, S-IC, and SII, were so large that they had to be transported by barge, from New Orleans, through the Gulf of Mexico, around Florida, and up the intracoastal waterway, to the launch site.

The spacecraft would take three days, and go through a number of maneuvers, to position itself for the moon landing. The ship, minus the Saturn V, had three primary sections, the Command Module "Columbia", where the crew lived during most of the trip, the service module, which contained oxygen, water, and electric power for the command module. The Service Module also housed the service propulsion system—the rocket engine that put the spacecraft into lunar orbit and later boosted it back toward Earth. This module was jettisoned just before reentry into the Earth's atmosphere. Finally, the craft that would set down on the Moon, the Lunar Module, "Eagle", or L.M. Astronauts Armstrong and Aldrin would move into the LM, while Michael Collins would remain on the Columbia, orbiting the Moon until the LM blasted off the Moon and rendezvousing back with the Command Module. At this point, with all three astronauts back on the Command Module, the L.M. would be programmed to crash into the Moon, as it could not return to Earth, and neither could the Service Module, which would provide fuel to boost the Command Module back home.

Ray could not begin to fathom the work needed to get to this point. The trials and tribulations, the many people needed to build and test these instruments and parts. It was said that 400,000 people were involved in putting these three men into space, and two men on the Moon. That massive workforce stretched across the U.S. and included engineers, scientists, mechanics, technicians, pilots, divers, seamstresses, secretaries and more who worked tirelessly behind the scenes to achieve those first lunar footsteps .

Some, hopefully, just a few, subscribed to the "Moon Landing Hoax" theory, that the landing was staged. Ray thought that if that was true, more people were able to keep their mouths shut for all these years, than in any other endeavor in history. It was ridiculous.

By now, the entire sun had lifted itself over the horizon. You could practically see it moving. Of course, it wasn't the sun moving so much as it was the Earth's rotation turning toward it. The Earth rotated today as it did every day. The same sun our ancient descendants saw. The same sun as the great explorers searched rose and fell as they reached for new lands, new places, sometimes, at great risk. The same sun that this man, Commander Armstrong and his two comrades would see as they their ship blasted its way through the Earth's gravity, into the frigid, cold atmosphere, and then the great void of space, to land on a spherical mass, just as the same explorers, workers and dreamers had looked up at and wondered "What is out there? Are we alone?" Perhaps those answers would not come in 1969, or 1978, but Ray hoped that someday, they would.

Ray didn't want to move a muscle until this man, this scientist, this astronaut, moved, and then finally, he did. Neil Armstrong turned to Ray and said "Hey, thanks for giving me a little peace and quiet." Ray answered, slyly, "A little 'Tranquility' huh?" The Commander nodded approvingly. Ray simply wanted to let the Commander know that he wasn't an idiot. He understood the man, as much as he might dare, the mission, and maybe it formed a brief, temporary understanding. Maybe, just maybe, a bond.

Neil Armstrong said to Ray. "Well, morning has broken, care to walk with me back to the shore?" How could Ray say no? He wouldn't, but he still could not take himself to conduct an interview, as it were. Ray saw this as a small but important gesture by the great man, a reward, for Ray giving him his much-needed space. His reprieve from the world stage. His temporary solace. His sanity. "So, how are the Boilermakers looking for the fall?" Ray escaped to the safety of college football. "Well, funny you should ask", said the Commander. "Do you know, in 1945, I watched Purdue beat a very good Ohio State team, and I decided at that point, to attend Purdue? I got a free ride under the Holloway Plan, and served in the Navy as part of the requirement, so that's how I really got here. We'll see if the

Boilermakers can beat the Buckeyes this fall". "Wow", said Ray, "that's a great story. Hope Ohio State can win". They didn't. Nor did they beat Michigan, but like in 1968, they had a respectable 8-2 record in a tough Big Ten Conference. Maybe it was a momentary reprise from the Commander's thoughts, and Ray thought even more of the man now that he knew he was a college football fan.

They reached the end of the pier, and the street. Ray said, "Mr. Armstrong, Good luck, sir." "What's your name, son?" the Commander asked. "It's Ray Stone, Sir", replied Ray. He felt like saluting but that would be over the top by anybody's estimation. "Well, Ray, thanks, and take care of yourself. Oh, here", the Commander said as he reached into his pocket. "A little souvenir". It was a coin, about the size of a half dollar. A commemorative Apollo 11 coin, featuring the faces of Armstrong, Aldrin, and Collins on the front, and the Apollo 11 Mission logo on the back, with an Eagle with olive branch about to land on the Moon. It probably could be bought for $5.00, but how many people had it handed to them by the first man to walk on the Moon?

Say it, Ray. Say it.

"Sir? That first step? That's going to be a great leap". Neil Armstrong stared at him for a long three seconds.

No....Ray did not say it. It was not for Ray to stick his nose into the annals of history. It was not his place, not his spotlight. Those words would be said.

Neil Armstrong walked across the street to a parked car, and drove away in seconds, and Ray was awestruck.

In almost seconds, Ray found himself in bed. Waking up, he walked downstairs to breakfast, where his Mom, Dr. Gene, and his sister, were having breakfast. "Eat before it's gone, Ray", said his Mom. "Oh, also, I hope you don't mind, but I had to go into your room while you were sleeping, and this was on the floor". His Mom handed him an Apollo 11 medallion. "Hey, Ray, let's see that", his Dad said. Realizing that Ray could have found a million places to buy it, he lost interest quickly, after studying it. "Nice" was all he said. Ray's sister grabbed it, and said "Always wasting your money, huh? Where did you get this?" Not that she really cared. Ray answered without missing a beat. "Neil Armstrong himself handed it to me." The truth was refreshing. His sister, as if also on cue, rolled her eyes and left the table to find something that was worthwhile to do.

Neil Armstrong, as history showed, and as Ray already knew, had his historic flight, the first step, and the iconic quote "That's one small step for (a) man, one giant leap for mankind", at 10:56 p.m. ET on July 20, 1969. Following their return to Earth and 18-day quarantine, the Astronauts embarked on a 38-day tour of the nation, including ticker-tape parades.

Neil Armstrong taught for years at the University of Cincinnati, and worked on other projects, and passed away on August 25th, 2012, following a heart by-pass operation. The reluctant American hero, as humble during life as he was, possibly, on that Cocoa Beach pier, will forever be associated with one of America's, and the world's, greatest moments.

IRON HORSE

Ray Stone was a football fan, always college. After all, he lived in Georgia. Sure, the Falcons played around 75 miles to the west, at Atlanta's Fulton County Stadium, at the southern lip of downtown Atlanta, home to both the baseball Braves and Falcons. The Falcons arrived as an expansion team in Atlanta in 1965, only eight years ago. He liked quarterback Steve Bartkowski, a heckuva good QB at Cal Berkeley, and a rising star in the NFL. The Falcons would see their first playoff season in 1978, but falter two games in, in what would come to be another futile attempt at championship greatness.

Ray loved the world of college football, the all-day festivities, the music, the tailgating, the crowds. Whether at Georgia, where he lived just two miles from campus, and where his dad, Dr. Eugene (Gene) Stone taught history, at LeConte Hall. Of course, both his Dad and Mom were Wisconsin-Madison grads, and while Mom seemed a little detached from it, Dr. Gene still had a thing for his beloved Badgers. Ray himself had been to the iconic Camp Randall Stadium, the site of a Union Army training base during the Civil War, and the namesake of the stadium. Ray liked how it was built in stages, like Georgia's Sanford Stadium, which would have a massive expansion following the big 1980 championship season. Ray, an Athens, GA resident, and likely, future Bulldog, still had somewhat of a dual loyalty, being that their Athens home was practically "Madison South". Dr. Gene sometimes, like Ray, took football to extremes. The "dark days", when Ray was around seven, took place when the Badgers lost 24 straight games.

Yes, Ray liked the interesting history behind both schools, blending sports with history. He liked that the Bulldogs played their first game in Sanford Stadium in 1929, against the Yale Bulldogs. Symbolism. Respect. Hard, fair play. Important things in the Stone household, where the honor of battle, of commitment, of loyalty was repeated regularly through many great stories of history.

Ray wasn't a big baseball fan. For him, it moved too slowly. There was no contact. Oh sure, you had the occasional collision between runner and fielder, but not like the crunching of bodies on every football play. Of course, baseball players could walk away from the game with fewer injuries, fewer illnesses. Right? Well, there were some exceptions, where good history was involved. There were the New York Yankees, once the Highlanders, who had won more World Series titles than any baseball team in the league. Heck, they were the defending champs in 1978, but it was July, and the Yanks were 14 games out. Even Ray, preparing for the Bulldogs opening game against Baylor in September, knew that the Bronx Bombers were already out of it.

The Yankees had enough history to fill a book, many books. From the Babe, to Gehrig, to DiMaggio and Mantle, there were a lot of colorful stories, and Ray liked reading colorful stories.

It was summer, and Ray had his job at Allen's the beloved hamburger joint off Prince Street, known around the world due to the Navy personnel at the nearby supply school, wearing the Allen's t-shirt in different ports. He wished he had a date, but that would be a big no. He went to the Clarke Central prom with a girl who also wanted to go, but nothing came out of it after that. While "I Just Want to be Your Everything" by Andy Gibb, played in the background, Ray danced the night away, though there would be no "after the prom" action. So, it was back to the drawing board and focus on work. He had one more year of high school left.

College was looking more and more like Georgia, but you never know. His dad had friends at Florida State, in Tallahassee, and Ray had gone down there, cruising along Apalachee Highway, and the family hitting the beach at St. George Island. Of course, there was Wisconsin, the sentimental favorite of the family, as both Mom and Dad attended. His dad also had ties to Rutgers in New Jersey, and suggested Ray at least apply there. "Where?" asked Ray.

It was a long day of flipping burgers, cleaning up, whatever the boss wanted, and the place was open until midnight on Saturday, and Ray was closing, so he didn't get out of the place until a few minutes after 1:00 AM. This was a summer vacation? Well, it was fine. Ray's parents always stressed the value of hard work and dedication, of loyalty and doing your best. They were kind of a "sassy" family. A lot of sarcasm and wit. An intelligent family if Ray could quietly boast. His sister was a math genius but sure didn't know her history like Ray. She dealt in facts and figures, so why not? "The past is the past" she would say. "But we have to know the past in order to be successful in the future!" Ray would say. His little sis Linda would, on cue, say "If you say, 'Those who do not learn history are doomed to repeat it' one more time, YOU'LL be history!"

But Linda would already be asleep when Ray drove down Prince Street, took a left on Pulaski, then another mile or so to the family driveway. The house was quiet. Athens wasn't a barrel of laughs in the summer. The campus was relatively empty, and even his Dad, Dr. Gene, was asleep. Ray couldn't watch The Tonight Show. No Johnny on Saturday night. Nothing at nearly 2:00 AM, so he was out in a flash.

Ray woke up, apparently, standing on a street corner. It was cold out. He looked at himself. He was wearing an overcoat and hat. Naturally, wherever he was or when, it was in the past. He hated this initial period of trying to determine where, and when, he was, but he had also gotten adept at keeping his wits long enough to figure something out. His clothing could have been anytime early to mid-20th century. Ray was no fashion designer or "clothing historian". He was standing on what was at least somewhat of a city street. No skyscrapers, but businesses. Cars going by. Okay, well at least there were cars. What he saw, old Cadillacs, but looking new, Buicks, made him think 1930s or perhaps 1940s. A quick glance to men walking the street. No military uniforms. Between 1942 and 1945, he wouldn't go 50 feet without seeing a handful of those. Just then, the situation got very easy for Ray. Across the street was a newsstand. One of those city kinds of stands he would see in New York City, with newspapers and magazines. He crosses the street and didn't even have to pick up anything and get yelled at by the proprietor ("Hey buddy, if you're going to read, you're going to buy). Well, he had his choice. Sitting on a low table in front of the stand was The New York Times, The New York Post, The Press, The Herald, The Tribune, The Telegram, The Mail and Express, The Evening News, The Commercial Advertiser, The World, The Sun, and The Journal. Holy mackerel. So many papers! How did they all survive? Well, in any event, they all shared one supremely important thing. They all had the date on top, and that date was January 15, 1940. A Monday. Ughh. It was 1940. Now what?

Ray walked across the street again. There was a diner of some kind. Mac's diner. Still, he didn't know where he was, except somewhere in New York, or awfully close to it. Inside, he saw a woman helping a man walk in and walk to a table. She seemed like she was in her 30s or so. The man wore a hat, and it was hard to see. He walked with a limp, and she was holding his arm. Finally, he sat down, and she bent over and kissed him. Ray could see through the windows, somewhat. Seconds later, she walked out. What that meant, he didn't know. He just had a feeling. He saw the woman exit the restaurant and walk down the street, but Ray couldn't tell who it was. It was time to walk in. He checked and saw that he had a few dollars in his pocket. Nice of the "dream Gods" or whatever was behind this, to put him in the right clothing and to give him a little cash.

Ray walked in and the place was nearly deserted. On the wall, the clock said 9:45. The breakfast crowd had no doubt thinned out and the place was almost empty. He was met by a waitress who said, "Sit down anywhere you want, hon". It took him only a few seconds but then he saw, in the corner, picking up a cup of coffee, very carefully, was Lou Gehrig. There was no mistake about it. He was reading a paper. Ray never got over the feeling of shock, and he had met, real or otherwise, some very famous people.

Ray sat down near Gehrig's table but didn't stare. In front of him was a very brief menu that said, "Mac's Diner, Riverdale-Bronx". The Bronx he knew. Riverdale, he had never heard of. He'd been in far worse situations. It was January 15th, 1940. It was cold, and that was Lou Gehrig, not in a baseball uniform, but a suit. Naturally, he could, and would, be wearing a suit away from the stadium, but now, it was 1940. Lou Gehrig was done playing baseball sometime in the spring of 1939. What he was doing now, Ray didn't know, but whatever it was, it wouldn't be for much longer.

Ray looked over the menu, bacon and eggs, 45-cents, coffee, 10-cents, 2 eggs, bacon toast and coffee, 65-cents. Sounded good to him. "What can I get ya, hon?" asked the waitress. "I'll have 2 eggs scrambled, bacon, toast and coffee". "Comin' up", the waitress said. A handwritten tag on her blouse said "Connie". Suddenly, a voice was heard in Ray's direction. "Good to get out of this cold, huh?" It was the Iron Horse himself. Ray was flustered, but maybe the former Yankee captain was used to that. He looked back over. "Yes, sir. It sure is". Ray then sat painfully through silence. It wasn't easy. Minutes seemed to go by. Finally, his food came. Then, suddenly, Lou Gehrig said, "Hey, have a seat over here if you'd like". No. Could Ray do that? How could he say no? It seemed uncommon from everything he read, that Lou Gehrig would invite strangers to come sit with him. Not that he wasn't pleasant, but he was shy. Well, Ray was a teenager. Hardly a threat. Raid said "Well, sure, I'd like to do that, if you're sure you don't mind". Ray needed to think about a conversation with this great but tragic figure.

Ray decided to be as straight as he could. Don't be starstruck, but yes, maybe a little. Be careful what else you say but don't deny knowing a little bit. Ray decided on his first sentence. "You probably don't get a lot of time to yourself, Mr. Gehrig. I mean, all the fans and all". "Well first, call me Lou. Secondly, since being out of the game, I haven't been around the stadium too much. Not like last year, when I sat with the team through the season and the series. But now, with the new job, it's really a lot different." Ray noticed that Gehrig was noticeably thinner than he remembered in pictures from his playing days, even in Stone and white photos, and Ray knew he had trouble walking, but sitting in a chair upright, he seemed at worst, a little unsteady.

Ray said, "Well it's really an honor to sit with you here. I never would have expected that." "Well,", said Lou, "don't give me the hero treatment, not now, anyway", and he smiled. "I'm a regular guy, more than you'll know. You look young, college aged. You don't go to Columbia by any chance, do you?" "No", said Ray. I'm in my last year of high school. I'm seventeen. "Yeah?" said Gehrig, the nasally New York accent clearly evident. "That's a good age. I hope you go on to college." Ray said, "Yes, my Dad teaches college down South". I'll be going somewhere. Gehrig was happy enough to gloss over the remark and move on from it. It was small talk. "That's good. That's very important. I wished I had finished at Columbia, but you know, things changed." "Well,", said Ray, "I know the Yankees were glad you left when you did." Gehrig laughed a little bit, "I suppose so". "What are you doing know?" asked Ray? He knew he had a city job of some sort, briefly, but couldn't remember what it was. "I got a job as the New York City Parole Commissioner". "Oh yeah", said Ray. I think I read about it, but I'm only up here visiting. Gehrig continued, "I've got to go visit a facility and meet with some inmates right after breakfast". "Do you like it?" asked Ray. Gehrig spoke, "I only just started at the beginning of this month. You know, I could have done better, if you know what I mean, with some personal appearances, speaking engagements, that sort of thing, but the mayor was kind enough to give me this offer, and it's a chance to be a public servant for a while." Ray said, "Well, good luck. I hope those meetings go well". Gehrig laughed, "Hey thanks. I'll bet the inmates hope they go well. I'm the guy that may decide if they're paroled or not, and really, I take it seriously".

Gehrig took all his jobs seriously. As a member of the New York Yankees, from 1923 to 1939, he took his playing seriously to the point that he may not have been the favorite player in the clubhouse, to the media, or even to fans, at least not at first. He didn't have the charisma of Babe Ruth. Everyone knew that, but by 1927, with what was considered perhaps the finest baseball team ever assembled, he had one of the greatest years a player has ever had, then, or since. Gehrig hit .373, with 218 hits: 101 singles, 52 doubles, 18 triples, 47 home runs, a then-record 175 RBIs (surpassing teammate Babe Ruth's 171 six years earlier), and a .765 slugging percentage.

Ray told the truth, "Well, Lou", the word "Lou" not rolling of Ray's tongue too well, as he simply had too much respect for the man, "determining if a man is going to stay in prison or go free is a pretty big deal".
"Exactly", expressed Lou. "That's what I thought when Mayor LaGuardia offered it". "LaGuardia?" Ray thought. "Like in the airport?" Hmmm, something Ray didn't know. He couldn't know everything.

"I saw you walking in with somebody. Will she be back? Have I taken her chair?" "Oh, no", said Gehrig. "That was my wife, Eleanor. She is running some errands in the neighborhood and will come back. My folks are coming over for dinner, and she always gets nervous about that". Ray knew the story this time. Gehrig was devoted to his mother. You might even say he was a "Momma's boy", though not to his face. This was a man, at least at one time, that resembled more of a fullback than a first baseman, and in fact, he played college football at Columbia. His mother was very strong-willed, but unfortunately, so was his wife, Eleanor, and they never got along. By now, it was probably out in the media somewhat, even in 1940, so Ray simply said "Ahh, the daughter-in-law and mother-in-law thing. A common story". Gehrig laughed, "You said it, buster. If you knew only half of it". They both laughed. Gehrig said, "You sure you're only seventeen? You're not a newspaper writer, are you?". Ray smiled, "Oh no, just up here visiting from out of state." Gehrig continued, "You a big baseball fan?" Ray said, "To be totally honest, I'm a bigger football fan, maybe because I live in Georgia where we have no professional team, but I've sure followed your career." "Well, that's nice of you to say", Gehrig said. Ray decided to have some fun, to see where it went. "Do you think there will ever be a major league team down south, or out west?" Gehrig enjoyed thinking about it, philosophically, like the student of the game he was. "I think, yes, some day, perhaps, if the crowds are big enough to sustain it, there might be a team somewhere down south, or out west. You know, we spend a lot of time in Florida at spring training and get good crowds, but we also wouldn't want to thin-out the talent in the league by having too many teams, but gradually, why not. The whole country should have the chance to see America's pastime, even if you're a football fan", Lou said with a broad smile. "But I'm a football fan, too", said Lou. "Carried the pigskin for the Lions at Columbia for a couple of years." Ray went further. "Well, maybe the Yankees would move down South or out west!" Ray said, making sure he knew that Lou knew he was joking. "Never happen", said Lou, smiling but also serious. Then he laughed. "Let the league send the Dodgers and Giants out west". Ray laughed, knowing more than Lou could or would know. "That's exactly what should happen," laughed Ray. "Who needs dem bums?" "Now that I like!" Lou said, and laughed. It seemed like the first time he had been laughing for a little while. He was turning out to be the person Ray always imagined him to be. A little serious, perhaps, but extremely…. what word is right? Decent. Yes, the word was decent.

Lou Gehrig wasn't the playful character in the clubhouse that other players might have been. He didn't stay out late, didn't carouse with the guys, didn't drink much, if at all. In fact, he didn't really date too much before he met Eleanor, and when he did date, it wasn't unusual for his own mother to sabotage it. But, in Eleanor, he had found a wonderful partner, one perhaps a little more outspoken than Lou, but perhaps that was exactly what Lou needed.

Eleanor Grace Twitchell was born on March 6, 1904 in Chicago. Hardly the recluse like her husband, Eleanor liked to get out on the town. Her father kept the family very comfortable before bad business deals and marital decisions led to him losing his wealth. Eleanor and Lou were married in 1933, for a short eight years, and she remained a widow for forty-three years.

The relationship between Eleanor and her in-laws, mainly her mother-in-law, was famously, and correctly, poor. At one point, Eleanor even called off their engagement due to the tension but reconciled soon after. It would likely have been tough for anybody to break the mother-son bond between Lou and Christina Gehrig. Some say it was due to the fact that three children had already died in childbirth, or as infants. Lou was the only one to make it to out of his childhood. Lou knew this as well and it was sure to have had an effect on him.

"Hey Lou", Ray said. "I know about that movie you did. Rawhide. I watched it." "Oh, said, Lou, so you were the one, huh?" Lou said, and laughed. "Did you know that I tried out for Tarzan once". "Really?" said Ray, who did not know. "Yes, I did. Well, sort of", laughed Lou. I sent some photos of myself dressed in a loin cloth." "No, you didn't?" joked Ray. "I certainly did" said Lou, "and the studio said, 'keep playing baseball'. Eleanor has wanted me to expand my horizons for when my baseball career was over. Well," Lou said, a little quieted, "it's over now". A few seconds of uncomfortable silence. "Lou, can I tell you something, as a fan?" "Yeah, sure, you can. We're practically friends now" said Lou. Ray knew how he wanted to phrase it. "A guy that hits a lifetime .340, with almost 500 homers, and plays in over 2,000 consecutive games, doesn't suddenly get into a massive slump unless there's something going on, something physical, you know? I'm a fan, and always knew it. Always, and so did most people." "Well, that's nice of you to say. I always knew it, too, but had no idea what it could be". It was at this point, from the articles and a book Ray had read about the Iron Horse, that Ray wanted to get something out of the way. "I've only heard a little bit about what you've got, the affliction, but I hope you can lick it". "Well, thanks. You probably read that I went up to the Mayo Clinic in Minnesota. Let me tell you, those doctors up there are great. Not only are they the best at what they do, they're swell fellas." Ray thought how 1940's that sounded, and he was pleased to hear it. "Like I've told other people, it's a form of infantile paralysis. I have a chance to get stronger and beat it. Maybe a 50-50 chance, and I'm working on it." "Well,", said Ray, "I'm sure pulling for you. Even if your playing days are over, you played for a very long time, in over 2,000 straight games". "2,130, actually" smiled Lou, "but who's keeping count?" "It'll never be broken, that streak", said Ray. "Well, it needs to be", said Lou. "I'm proud to have it, but baseball needs to march on, get better, and some day, it should be broken. It'll be good for baseball." "Well, I just don't see it". With that remark, Ray was speaking the truth, because the Oriole's Cal Ripken Jr. wouldn't break Gehrig's record until September 6, 1995, over fifty years later.

"Say, how was you breakfast", asked Lou. "You know, I live right on Delafield, just three blocks from here, so I know the chef. If you had a problem, we'll get him right over here." "Oh no", said Ray "It was fine. It's pretty hard to ruin bacon and eggs." "You know", said Lou, "I've been trying forever to get them to put picked eels on the menu, like my mother makes". "Pickled eels?" said Ray. "Well, enjoy that without me!". Lou laughed, "Oh, no, they're great".

"Well, Lou, and you know I'd be a lot more comfortable calling you Mr. Gehrig", Ray said, I think I'll get going. It has been an honor having breakfast with you. Best of luck with your job on the Parole Board, and I wish the very best in recuperating from this lousy thing you have to deal with." "Hey, thanks a lot. I know I've got a fighting chance to beat it, and with my doctor's help, I'm going to do it." Ray said, "If anybody can, it'll be you. The movie studios might need you to do another western". Lou laughed, flashing a big grin. "That'll be the day".

Ray walked out of the diner, and for several minutes, roamed the streets in the Riverdale section of the Bronx. He took in the scenery. It wasn't everyday that he roamed the streets of New York, in 1940.

He walked into a small park and sat on a bench. Suddenly very tired, he breathed in and felt himself tearing up just a little bit but didn't want any passersby to notice. Like anytime he bears witness to people, an unknown, or as in this case, the very famous, he tries to understand them, to "get into their heads" a little bit if he can, for the sake of understanding the history. It's never going to change anything or to upset the situation. In this case, what could Ray possibly have said to Lou Gehrig that he already didn't know. Despite not being a baseball fan, he read-up on Lou Gehrig, because he was a fan of the man. He was one of his personal heroes, and today, he wasn't let down. Gehrig seemed a kind, proud man. Once very powerful and sure of himself on the ballfield, if not off it. Stories of his clumsiness, his awkwardness in life were a little bit overblown, even if Ray wasn't watching Lou in public situation besides sitting at a restaurant table. It was a little up in the air what Gehrig knew about his illness, Amyotrophic Lateral Sclerosis, or ALS, a disease so unknown that his celebrity caused the public to adopt the replacement name "Lou Gehrig's disease". Ray was unsure when that moniker took hold, but he's certain that Lou would hate it.

The books and articles Ray read said that the highly trained doctors at Rochester, Minnesota's famed Mayo Clinic saw the signs of ALS on Lou Gehrig quickly, though made sure that he received a thorough series of tests and examinations. The big question was "what was he told?". Based on his wife's own memoirs, the doctors told her everything, but held back when telling Lou. His wife said that he would suffer enough with the physical changes without the mental anguish. Lou had a stiff upper lip, telling people that his chance was "50-50", even up to the end, but in the case of Lou Gehrig, his changes came very quickly. His weight, his ability to walk and function properly, changed, seemingly, by the month, week, and even, sometimes, the day. Yet, he remained very lucid, very clear of mind, to the end, according to the stories. Perhaps that was not the best of circumstances, but what was? Some say that the number of concussions Gehrig had brought on the disease, but who's to know? Even the experts, years later, without an autopsy, which he did not have, wouldn't be able to say.

Ray suddenly found himself in a familiar position, in bed, staring across the room to the Georgia Bulldogs and Wisconsin Badgers pennants on the wall. He envisioned two more he would have liked to place there now. The familiar Yankees logo, that stitched baseball with bat forming part of the Yankees "k", the stars and stripes hat, the script writing on the baseball. So American, so patriotic, which was right up Ray's alley. Of course, don't tell the fans and players of other teams that only the Yankees were patriotic, because just two years later, the war would break out, and many of the players would be donning other uniforms, delaying their "games" to fight for their nation. The other pennant Ray could imagine, was from Columbia, the blue lion. It made Ray, a lover of all things collegiate, including the fight songs, think about that tune he liked:

Roar, Lion, Roar
And wake the echoes of the Hudson Valley
Fight on to victory evermore
While the sons of Knickerbocker
Rally 'round Columbia, Columbia!
Shouting her name forever
Roar, Lion, Roar
For Alma Mater on the Hudson shore!

Maybe "Columbia Lou" wasn't what came to mind when thinking of the Ironhorse, but Ray, at this time, made it a little more relevant in his mind, because that's how Ray thought. For Lou, perhaps it began at New York's Commerce High School, where Lou became a star, and his team travelled to Chicago, to the great Wrigley field, to play a championship game against Lane High School of Chicago, in 1920. With the score 8-6 in favor of Commerce, 17-year-old Gehrig hit a towering shot, over the right field wall, and onto the street. A grand slam. The papers touted him as "the Babe Ruth of the high schools". Speaking of the great Bambino, the ever-so-beloved and popular player for the Yankees, Gehrig could never quite step out of his shadow, though he was an integral part of the duo of Gehrig and Ruth, batting 3-4 in the lineup for so many years, striking fear into the hearts of opposing pitchers. It wasn't enough that Gehrig was a model player, always playing hard, never complaining, despite the many injuries, wrangled, sometimes broken fingers and other ailments that would have put a lesser man on the bench. He kept playing. He could have held out for more money. His wife certainly pushed him to do that, but inevitably, he settled much of the time for what was offered. He didn't want to disappoint management, his teammates, the fans, or himself, by missing any spring season games and holding up his progress as a player.

Ruth left the Yankees in 1934, and by 1936, another charismatic player, Joe DiMaggio joined the team, and Gehrig played second fiddle again, in the eyes of many of the fans. The player from San Francisco quickly became the fan favorite, and played like it, too.

Babe Ruth and Lou Gehrig had strikingly different personalities, and for different reasons, they didn't always get along as people thought they might. Of course, any book would go into that. Some say their wives had words, which spread to the men, and at one point, they were close to fisticuffs one day in the locker room. But, when Gehrig played for the last time, in April of 1939, plans were soon put into place for a "Lou Gehrig Appreciation Day" during a Yankees doubleheader, on July 4, 1939, and over 61,000 fans showed up. Between games, in what is now so very famous, Gehrig was awarded many gifts, while New York notables, including Ruth, spoke on his behalf. Never the one to want to be in the limelight, Gehrig, uncomfortable but very moved, was urged by his manager, Joe McCarthy, to say a few words. Those few words became one of the greatest speeches ever recited in the world of sports, or anywhere else:

"For the past two weeks you have been reading about a bad break. Today I consider myself the luckiest man on the face of this earth. I have been in ballparks for seventeen years and have never received anything but kindness and encouragement from your fans.

When you look around, wouldn't you consider it a privilege to associate yourself with such fine-looking men as are standing in uniform in this ballpark today? Sure I'm lucky. Who wouldn't consider it an honor to have known Jacob Ruppert? Also, the builder of baseball's greatest empire, Ed Barrow? To have spent six years with that wonderful little fellow, Miller Huggins? Then to have spent the next nine years with that outstanding leader, that smart student of psychology, the best manager in baseball today, Joe McCarthy? Sure, I'm lucky.

When the New York Giants, a team you would give your right arm to beat, and vice versa, sends you a gift—that's something. When everybody down to the groundskeepers and those boys in white coats remember you with trophies—that's something. When you have a wonderful mother-in-law, who takes sides with you in squabbles with her own daughter—that's something. When you have a father and a mother who work all their lives so you can have an education and build your body—it's a blessing. When you have a wife, who has been a tower of strength and shown more courage than you dreamed existed—that's the finest I know.

So, I close in saying that I might have been given a bad break, but I have an awful lot to live for. Thank you."

Amazingly, there exists no known recording of this entire speech. Only portions of it. Ray had read it and had seen the available recording on TV once or twice. Who didn't know the "luckiest man" speech? It didn't come up during Ray's encounter, or dream, or whatever "too real to be a dream" encounter that Ray had. That he ALWAYS had, and why should it? Everybody knew it. Ray surmised that Lou was a simple man in many ways. He sensed that Lou thought nothing of having a light conversation with a young man. Lou remembered when he was a boy, no doubt, at Commerce High. Maybe too shy to ask a girl out on a date. A boy with a swing like a man, but in other ways, a boy up until his death. Yet, a man who could enjoy operas in German, the native tongue of his parents, which Gehrig understood. A well-spoken man who simply wanted to please people, who didn't like taking shortcuts in life, or advantage of people. A hero? He would say "no". Not a hero like Audie Murphy, much smaller than Lou, a skinny kid from Texas with nothing, who would become America's most decorated solider in just a few short years. Lou wouldn't get to see that. Yet, a hero in other ways, was Lou, not just for his play, his incredible baseball statistics, but in the way he handled the prospect of death. Surely, Ray thought, as have so many others, that Lou knew he was going to die. That he knew before he left the grounds of the Mayo Clinic. That Eleanor knew, and most likely, his family, his friends, they knew. If they didn't know when he began to struggle at the plate, and most didn't, they would later know, and those closest to him, they would surely know as they saw this great man, this rock, this man too muscular to play Tarzan, perhaps, was wasting away, due to the terrible, cruel affects of ALS, the disease later to bear his name.

During his "slump", Gehrig took a lot of heat. Heat from the press, the fans, perhaps even the players. "Why was Gehrig still in the lineup?" "He's hurting the team". Nobody was more aware than Gehrig himself, but slumps happen. Still, Gehrig, in the few accounts available, knew that this time, it was different. His bat was meeting the ball just fine, but he had no power. The ball wasn't travelling like it did before. No more line-drive homers, a Gehrig trademark. It wasn't just a slump. It was something more. Something worse, but what? Ray wondered, he had always wondered this, "How did the naysayers feel now? Now that they knew the great man was dying?" Is it fair to blame them? New York is a tough sports town. "Put up or shut up".

Gehrig "put up", alright. Besides the celebrated consecutive games streak, he had a lifetime batting average of .340. number 16 on the all-time list. Gehrig hit 493 home runs, with 1,995 runs batted in. He was an all-star seven consecutive years, and a member of six world championship teams. Many years later, in 1997, a "greatest of all time" team was assembled, featuring the likes of Honus Wagner, Babe Ruth, and Johnny Bench. Gehrig was the first baseman. The best combination of hitting and yes, even fielding, that the game had ever seen.

Lou Gehrig kept his job from January 1940, to around May 1941, when his condition was so severe, that he couldn't make it into work. He died, peacefully, at his Riverdale, Bronx home, on June 2nd, 1941, at 10:10 PM. Babe Ruth and his wife immediately came to the Gehrig home, and he wept at his open casket viewing just a few days later. Gehrig died seventeen days before his 38th birthday.

Only a year later, a movie depicting the life of Lou Gehrig, "Pride of the Yankees" hit the screens, featuring one of Ray's favorite actors, Gary Cooper. It quickly became a fan favorite, and movie-goers favorite, even if some of the movie's facts were changed, a common practice for the movies. Even the iconic "Luckiest Man" speech was redone, but it didn't seem to matter, as the key passages were there. Who didn't cry, Ray thought, when that speech on the great wide screen was finished, and Gary Cooper's Lou Gehrig slowly turned away and headed for the tunnel leading to the clubhouse, to the strains of the song played so often in the movie? The last thing we hear, the last piece of dialogue, came from the umpire, off screen, shouting "play ball". Life goes on. Baseball goes on, just like the love theme in the movie, the great Irving Berlin theme, "Always". "Not for just an hour, not for just a day, not for just a year, but always".

ALS, or amyotrophic lateral sclerosis, is a motor neuron disease. that results in the progressive loss of motor neurons that control voluntary muscles. ALS is the most common type of motor neuron disease. Early symptoms of ALS include stiff muscles, muscle twitches, and gradual increasing weakness and muscle wasting. The affected muscles are responsible for chewing food, speaking, and walking. Motor neuron loss continues until the ability to eat, speak, move, and finally breathe, is lost. ALS eventually causes paralysis and early death, usually from respiratory failure. More than 80 years since the passing of Lou Gehrig, there is still no cure. The average survival from onset to death is two to four years.

At Yankee stadium, there resides "Monument Park", an open-air museum, with plaques remembering Yankee greats. On Lou Gehrig's plaque is an inscription that reads, "Henry Louis Gehrig. A man, a gentleman, and a great ball player".

A RAY OF HOPE

Ray was invited to a party over on the east side of town, just off Barnett Shoals Road, in enemy territory. Of course, that was Cedar Shoals High School, the new school, built just six years ago. The Jaguars were the arch enemy of the Clarke Central High Gladiators, but Ray didn't really go into all that, and he felt that the big rivalry, the "Classic City Championship" game held every year, was not so much of a big deal. He had some friends scattered around town, and that's why he was at this party, only a few blocks from the high school he was "supposed" to hate, but really, didn't.

On his way over, down Broad Street in the center of town, cutting through the south side of campus, past the arena and football practice field, and past the College of Education, and onto East Campus Road, then College Station Road, the busy campus quickly came to an end and the land turned into pastures, open fields, some land used by the University for agricultural purposes until he came across Barnett Shoals Road, where neighborhoods popped up, near the school. Once on Barnett Shoals Road, he turned into the neighborhood where Ricky Stillman lived, one of his longtime Athens friends from little league years ago, and other summer activities. His parents both worked at the University, not an unusual situation in this college town. Just a couple of blocks from the home, in a steady, cold drizzling December rain, he noticed, just barely, a body sitting on the curb. It was 8:30 PM, very dark considering the winter month. Unusual, but nothing to really write home about. Probably waiting for a ride, and certainly, none of Ray's business. He kept driving the two or three blocks to Ricky's house, parked, and got out. Several other cars were already there, either in the driveway or along the quiet street.

The kids at the party weren't much different than his Clarke Central friends. A tape machine was playing Gerry Raferty's "Baker Street", with the screaming sax intro and cool lyrics:

"Winding your way down on Baker Street
Light in your head and dead on your feet
Well, another crazy day

One more year, Ray thought. Out of high school. Life would change, even if he remained in Athens, Georgia, the "classic city", named of course for the cradle of western civilization and birthplace of Democracy, in Greece. So much that Americans took for granted, Ray, with his appreciation of history, surmised. High School was, easy, just like the lyrics. One more year and you'll be happy. Ray was happy. No worries there, and there would be no "cryin'". Maybe for others, not for Ray. It was okay, and the song was great, one of many played that night.

The kids talked about sports, at least the boys. It was December 9th, 1978, just a week after Buck Belue, the Georgia Freshman quarterback, helped lead the Bulldogs to a thrilling, come-from-behind win over the hated Georgia Tech Yellowjackets. It was especially great to see, after Georgia Tech took a commanding 20-point lead. Redemption was great. No crying, but there might have been!

Yes, that game was a super performance by the "Dawgs" much like Superman, the movie, from actor Christopher Reeve. Reeve did the part justice. Just the first in a trilogy, he was that humble, yet strong man from the planet Krypton, and Gene Hackman played the perfect foil as Lex Luther. Nobody at this party would have any idea that this fine actor would suffer a terrible accident in 1995, thrown from a horse and paralyzed. He would become an inspiration to so many before succumbing to his injuries at the young age of 52. During his life, he would speak up for the less fortunate, those suffering like him, and those suffering from other ailments and conditions.

They talked about Animal House, those misfit Delta's at the fictitious Faber College, and their rivalry with the prestigious Omegas.

Somebody had suggested that this party be a "toga" party, like in the movie, but with the parents upstairs, there was no liquor (supposedly), and no togas. No, and there was no "Otis Day and the Knights" as in the movie, but there was a rendition of shout, with the partiers, even without the booze (supposedly), going "a little bit lower now, a little bit lower now", along with the song, and singing "SHOUT" at the appropriate time. They talked about Grease, and how "hot" Olivia Newton John was. Of course, the girls liked John Travolta just fine, and why shouldn't they. They WERE girls, right, and he was a nice-looking guy that could dance. I mean, Ray wouldn't know about good-looking guys. He WAS a guy, naturally. Somebody said that the studio wanted to film Animal House at the nearby University of Georgia campus, but it was denied. It was widely known anyway that UGA had its share of parties. I mean, who didn't already go to some of the parties. The high school girls, seniors now, especially had an easy time going to a frat party, or even a bar. After all, Freshman college guys were just a year older. Big deal. This was Athens, home of the B52s and REM, and Ray's favorite band "Phil and the Blanks". With the right connections, you might find yourself at the B&L Warehouse, T.K. Harty's Saloon, or at one of the many fraternity or sorority houses along stately Milledge Avenue, just steps from Ray's beloved Clarke Central High School. Ray was a little "straightlaced", he thought. A straight-A student with a love of history, and a Professor-father, Ray wasn't the "big man on campus" in high school, so he knew he certainly wouldn't be on a big college campus, whether that was UGA, or maybe Wisconsin, where his parents attended and met. Certainly, even Madison, WS had its parties. Ray wasn't exactly a ladies-man, either, but he knew one thing, he liked girls. Nothing wrong with his hormones there, and he figured he'd have a larger pool of girls to choose from in college. As far as this party went, the kids didn't pair-off to go make out. It was rather uneventful, and things began to wind down after 11:00 and he decided he would go. He wasn't the first to leave, nor the last, so he figured he could bow out gracefully.

A cold rain began to fall from the sky as Ray pulled out in his less than glamorous 1973 Ford Pinto. Earned with his money he made at Allen's Bar and Grill off of Prince Avenue, in the "Normaltown" section of Athens, Ray was happy to have four-wheeled transportation. He set off for home.

Ray thought of where he might be in a year, once again. He was a happy kid, he reasoned. He had a few friends, an occasional date. His dad, always the calm, studious type, nevertheless did a little boxing in school, much to Ray's surprise, and they had a speed bag and heavy bag in the basement. It was so humorous to see his dad work the bags. This guy with the tweed jackets, skinny, sweating. It just didn't fit him, his personality, but Ray also knew that some things weren't as they seemed in life. In people.

Long ago, Ray's dad gave his son a few lessons. Boxing pointers. He spoke. "Ray, I want you to use your brain to get ahead in life. Study hard. However, there are sometimes situations you may have to fight your way out of. Try to avoid it but just in case, and so you can have a little piece of mind, I want you to know at least the rudimentary skills of boxing." Just the fact that his dad, Dr. Gene, said "rudimentary skills" while discussing a way to smack the hell out of a guy, was different, but that was his dad.

So, every so often, they would punch the bag. Dr. Gene would teach him that if somebody couldn't hit you, they couldn't hurt you, so he taught him the art of ducking and weaving, counter punching, and combination punching. "When you punch, never waste an opportunity to hit with a combination, while your opponent has yet to recover". It sounded like he was teaching history, or art. Maybe boxing WAS an art, in a way. There was an artistic side of many things. Ray was never great at this thing, but his dad said that occasionally, a couple of times a month, get down into the basement and hit the bag. It was a good cardio workout as well as good preparation, good insurance, "just in case". Well, that "just in case" time came when he was fourteen, three years prior. Here was Ray, mostly quiet, very introspective kid, interested in history and in protecting his grade A average, at the mall one night, minding his own business, when a kid he knew, a kid with a bad reputation, decided this was the night to pick on Ray. A couple of insults, as a test. The bully was watching. How would Ray react? Would he get the desired response? Fear? Embarrassment? That was the goal. Eventually, if the bully decided and was egged on, a shove in the face, a push to the ground. Physical punishment wasn't the goal. It usually wasn't. Humiliation was the goal.

This was all new to Ray. He had escaped this so far. There were "nerdier" kids. "Goofier" kids. Ray was exceedingly average. An easy target? Maybe, but there were easier ones. A distinguishing characteristic. A look, a behavior. Something to make the victim different. Vulnerable. This night would be the night Ray was chosen, nonetheless. Simply because the bully in this situation felt like it.

The words started. Stupid words. Words meant to tear-down. Nothing unusual. Words to feminize Ray. That was always a good tactic for the bully, for after all, young men were trying to be men. Real men. It was well-understood that being compared to a woman was degrading. Not that the boys didn't like the girls, mind you, but to have the appearance or characteristics of a girl was "unmanly". Ray, once again, was a normal kid, but that didn't matter. What mattered was that the bully had an audience. You know, to build himself up from whatever discomfort he had in his life. Whatever void he had missing in his own life, whatever punishment from home or in his mind he was suffering, that he had to tear down others.

The kid followed Ray and his two friends. Ray tried to ignore him, but that only escalated matters. We all know where this was heading. When the words didn't work, the bully, not wishing to face embarrassment himself, would have to turn physical. A little slap in the face, a shove to the ground. Anything to achieve the main goal. Humiliate your victim. Yes, it felt good. It removed his own pain. Tear down your victim to build yourself up.

The bully and his entourage, themselves weak in character, but not wanting to be on the other side of this, the victim's side themselves, which might happen if they didn't "go along", laugh at the right times, perhaps even take a little swipe to the victim, continued to follow. Finally, the moment of truth came. Ray didn't play football; he was a girl and other assorted negative things. Finally, the bully got physical, "What's the matter? Afraid to fight?" Yes, Ray, WAS afraid, but bravery without fear isn't bravery at all. They go together. The kid shoved Ray. Sometimes that ended it, but often, it took another series. Ray pushed back. "Fine" the bully thought. What I wanted. "Really?" said the bully. "Big mistake, little Ray". He approached Ray, and Ray finally, after years, came to realize the term "muscle memory" and "habit-forming" that his dad had said ad-nauseum to him. The kid reeled back, practically in slow motion, as if Ray would just "take it". "This wasn't a boxer", thought Ray. Just a bully. It was easier than he ever realized. The bully swung. Ray ducked and weaved like he'd done hundred of "wasteful" times before. Ray punched into the totally exposed, softer-than-expected belly of the bully. All the air went out of the bully, and his hands, both of them, immediately grabbed his stomach, an involuntary action that Ray expected. The fight was already over at this point, but Ray remembered what Dr. Gene said, "Never waste an opportunity for a combination." With both hands clutching his stomach, the face was now totally exposed. "It really works", thought Ray, later. Like science. It's predictable. The Stone family liked things that were planned, thought-out, scientific, predictable. Measurable. Ray hit this kid hard in the nose. It cracked. It bled. The kid went down in a heap. Security came and it didn't take long for the facts to come out. In fact, the security detail knew the bully. Think this was the first time? Do you think bullies don't continue to bully? Well, that depends. Suddenly, his little entourage was much braver, not so afraid to speak up. The kid teased Ray, wouldn't leave him alone. Picked on him, shoved him, then took a swing at him and Ray simply defended himself. This was 1975. Ray would not be punished for defending himself, and the bully got medical care, we suppose. Ray left the scene, but the "scene" didn't leave him. No, the story followed Ray back to school. It always does. The legend of Ray Stone was born.

No, Ray didn't exactly become a legend, but Ray was never bothered again. He was never bothered before, and there were certainly some big kids that could take care of Ray, but they were decent kids and had no interest in picking on anybody. The bully at the mall certainly had no interest in picking on Ray again. Ray told his parents, and his Dad was proud, no matter how hard he tried to conceal it. "Nobody should be bullied, Ray, whether they are prepared to defend themselves or not. Words are much better. Walking away is better". "Then why did you teach me how to box?" asked Ray. "Because sometimes, you have no choice, but there are better ways to fight. I'm sorry you had to go through that, the name-calling for no sound reason. Remember how you felt so that you can be understanding of others." Always a teaching moment when it came to his dad.

Ray drove slowly, still raining, two blocks away, just before he got to Barnett Shoals Road, sort of the main thoroughfare in this part of the city. He drove past somebody on the curb and kept going. It took him a few seconds. "Wait", he thought. "That was the same person from three hours ago". Ray wondered now. This person, in dark clothing, head down, wasn't waiting for a ride. Something was going on. Ray kept driving and got onto Barnett Shoals Road. It was about 11:45. He had a midnight curfew. He didn't feel right. "Ray, turn around, damn it". It gnawed at him. Something was wrong. He knew it but didn't want to bother with it. But if he went home, he wouldn't stop thinking about it. Maybe it would bring him trouble. Maybe this person was another bully. He got lucky once. Maybe he would be drawn into something he would regret. Why look for trouble? Ray realized; it was all about him. He thought himself at the party as a pretty lucky kid. No real trouble. Parents that loved him, that provided the right amount of discipline. Explained things to him. Let him be himself but pushed him to be the best Ray he could be. Would THEY want him to stop? He didn't know. They also wanted him to avoid trouble. Ray was almost eighteen. The time to always wonder what your parents would say couldn't go on forever. Time to make your own decisions. Ray turned around.

He went back to the neighborhood. The rain was still coming down, in a soft drizzle, but a cold one. Not at all comfortable. Georgia or not, it was north Georgia, and colder than people thought it might be in a Southern town. Wet and cold, and you didn't sit on a curb for at least three hours unless something was wrong.

There he was. It was a he, Ray could tell, behind the jacket, not nearly a warm-looking one for this weather, almost as if the person wanted to be cold, wet, and miserable. He slowed down but parked about 100 feet away, so as not to startle this person. He hopes that was the right thing to do. He might have to make a quick escape.

Ray got out of his Pinto and slowly walked toward the person. The view became clearer. He looked like another teenager. His head was down. Ray spoke up "Hey, excuse me, umm, are you okay?" No answer. Oh, this person heard just fine. Ray tried again, a different approach, "I, uh, saw you like three hours ago, when I drove into the neighborhood, and you were here then. Why are you sitting in the rain? I mean it's cold and wet out. Can I help you".

Silence. Ray didn't know what to do. Well, he didn't seem to be physically hurt. He wasn't hit by a car. Ray was nervous about approaching any closer. "Well,", Ray said, "I'm sorry if something is wrong, but if I can't help, I guess I should be going. I'm supposed to be home by midnight. I hope everything is okay." What else could Ray do, but he walked away slowly, in case this boy, that's what he was now, this teenaged boy, might say something, and that's what happened, barely within earshot. "What the hell can you do to help me?" came the response. Ray didn't know what to say. "Well, I don't know. What's wrong? Something must be wrong?" "Yeah, Einstein, good deduction", came the response, but Ray knew it wasn't personal. Ray started to feel just from this one sentence that this was probably a bright kid. Maybe he went to Cedar Shoals High School. I mean, in this neighborhood, that was the public school. Ray tried a new approach. "Hey, you must go to Cedar Shoals. I go to Clarke Central but I'm friends with Ricky Stillman, and he had a party right down the street. Do you know Ricky, and maybe Sharon Locke, Karen Simpson, Jimmy McDonald?" The face looked up, "Yeah, I know them, but they don't give a damn about me". At least Ray was getting him to talk.

Ray had some experience, in his dreams, or whatever it was, in getting people to discuss their problems, and this was a boy with a problem. Who doesn't have problems, but does everybody have somebody to listen? "Wait, Ray. This wasn't a dream. This wasn't the past. This was now. This was home. This really is life". Well, he thought he should start listening. "Look", said Ray. "I'm Ray Stone and I'm seventeen and I'm a senior at Clarke Central, like I said. I don't know what's wrong, but you can tell me, and I'll listen. I don't know if I can help you until I know what's wrong, and maybe I can't help you, but I promise not to give you any crap about it. I know what it's like to be picked on."

"You don't know CRAP", was the response. Loudly, like it was bottled up for three hours. "Have you been picked on every day for years, and when you thought you had only your parents to go to, they tell you you're a freak?" Ray didn't answer right away, because he thought there would be more coming, and there was. "I'm sick of it. Sick of not being able to be myself, whatever that is, sick of bullies, sick of my school, sick of my life." Then, Ray noticed something glimmering in his hand, a light that bounced off of it from a streetlamp. It was a gun. "Hey", Ray said. "Why do you have a gun". "Oh, you see that?" the kid answered. "I took it from my father's closet. I knew it was there. My life isn't worth living, but maybe I should use it on you, first", and he pointed it at Ray. Just like in the movies, Ray dove to the ground. He could feel himself shaking. "WHOA!! C'mon man" Ray hollered. Put that damn thing down. Just when Ray thought he might be helping somebody, when he turned his car around despite his misgivings, his instincts were totally wrong. "Keep driving, Ray". No, Ray, the hero, would once again save the day. Once again offer his little tidbits, his little gathering of words to help get John Adams back to his senses or give Lou Gehrig some respite from his troubles. Well, this was NO dream, and he was now going to pay for it with his life!

"I'm sorry", came the response, then, the tears, and a quiet, yet very painful sobbing. Ray was saddened at this tortured soul, and indeed, he was tortured about something, but self-preservation came first. "Okay, okay, you're sorry, but put the gun down! Move it away from you a couple of feet" The boy didn't answer but threw the gun onto the grass. He had no intention of using that gun on Ray or anybody else. In fact, he probably wouldn't even know how. He had never used a gun before. Ray had used guns, but his dad never used them growing up in Chicago, and in this hunting-happy land of Georgia, Ray had only shot them a few times, at camp. With friends that hunted.

Ray tried a totally new approach. Now, he was invested and no longer believed he could be shot and killed. Ray had, just maybe, an edge, an advantage, some knowledge, real or otherwise. He had his "events", his dreams into the past. Ray always wondered why. "Why me? Is this real? Am I being tested?" It gave Ray a sense, at times, of karma, as unscientific as that was, that maybe people were placed into situations for a reason. This kid, whatever his problem was, was disappointed by people in his life. People that perhaps he gave his trust to, only to be disappointed.

Ray approached the young man. "Look" he said, quietly. "You don't know me. I'm different than a lot of kids. I've listened to people. Maybe I'm here for a reason. Maybe I can't help you but tell me what's wrong. I mean, it's midnight, and if I'm gonna get my ass kicked by my parents, I've got to give them a damned good reason."

Ray added something, for a twist, "because, as usual, it's all about me".

Somehow, that last line, dripping with sarcasm, seemed to work, at least a little. A tiny crack in the armor this boy, and he WAS still a boy, had built around himself. "Yeah", he smiled, faintly. "It's about you. I get that." He looked at Ray, and he did something he didn't ever think he could do again, he put himself at risk. "I got into a fight with my parents tonight". "Well", said Ray, that happens to almost everybody. "No, you don't understand", he went on. "Wait" said Ray. At least tell me your name, okay. "Fine", I'm Todd Miller, and yeah, I do go to Cedar Shoals. I'm a Junior. I'm sixteen. I can't wait to get out of here, forever. I'm going to attend Georgia Tech in two years and then move away forever". "Okay, great" said Ray. "Thanks, Todd. Keep going". Todd continued, but slowly. "My parents, especially my dad, basically told me I was a freak. He was ashamed of me". "Did he really call you that? A freak?" "No, said Todd, be he may as well have. It's what he meant.", he said sarcastically, "and why should he be any different. It's not like I haven't heard that constantly in school every other day." "But why?" asked Ray. "You don't seem like a freak to me". "You know what, Ray? I don't know what I am. Maybe I am a freak. Maybe I'm not normal, but I'm me." "Well", said Ray, "you'll have to tell me more so I can understand. I mean, am I going to be shocked?" "You mean tell you so you can give me the same crap everybody else does?" "I won't", said Ray, and Ray meant it. "Well, I've heard it all, anyway. You'd just be one more." Todd took a long, deep, breath, and let it out. Boy, he needed to do that. "My mother caught me with a boy". "With a boy?" Ray already seemed to get it, but just didn't expect it. "Yeah, do I have to spell it out for you?" "No" Ray said, hesitantly. "I understand. You're gay". "Einstein delivers again" came Todd's response. Ray tried something. "Again, with the sarcasm. Do you know my sister?" "Why?" said Todd. "Oh, you'd fit in with my family, with the sarcasm. We live on it." "I wouldn't fit in with anybody" came the reply.

This was new territory for Ray. He actually only HEARD this new meaning for homosexuality a couple of years before. He heard friends calling somebody gay, and Ray thought, "I don't get it. What's so funny about that?" Well, they explained to the dimwitted Ray, what gay now meant, and that the subject of their discussion, their victim, wasn't "gay". It was meant to be an insult, to be demeaning. Now Ray understood, and it wouldn't be the first time the word, now with its new meaning was meant to belittle, sometimes among friends teasing each other, but any way you looked at it, it was not at all a compliment.

As Ray moved on from this "awakening" life went on. Nobody talked about being gay. He had always known the word "homosexuality" and of course, "homo" was tossed around in an extremely demeaning way. Ray never used it. Never thought about it. Was taught many times from his parents about other words, words like "dignity", "respect", "honor", "courtesy". He wouldn't do anything to destroy a person's dignity, but when his friends made these new, these "gay" jokes, did Ray laugh? Yes, at times, Ray, the dignified person of character, the nice guy, laughed.

Again, life went on, with barely a whisper about anything "gay". Certainly, nobody in public life, in entertainment, sports, or politics was gay. Nobody ever admitted it. There were whispers, perhaps, allegations. It was always a "dirty little secret", but let's be clear, it wasn't Ray's world. He never really thought about it. All he knew, had he thought about it, was that he liked girls. He had always liked girls. He never even thought about it. It just WAS. It was part of him. It was normal and natural.

Ray spoke once again to Todd. "Todd, I don't care if you're gay. You seem like a nice guy and you deserve to be treated with respect". "It's not a disease, Ray. It's not a sickness, but my parents, my dad, said it was wrong, he was disappointed in me. It made me sick to my stomach." "Todd", Ray said. "I feel that this is new territory for me. I don't understand it, but I'd like to. It's just hard for me, but you know, there ARE people who are confused but are kind". "I haven't met any". "Well", answered Ray, "maybe it starts now".

Ray had never met a gay person. Oh, perhaps he had met several, but unknowingly, and, he supposed, that was the point. The colonials had one insult after another imposed on them by the British. Stone people, and they did talk about civil rights often, one insult after another, more than one-hundred years after the abolishment of slavery by the 13th Amendment, on January 31, 1865. But, gay rights never did. It just never came up, but it was history also, but in a different, far more personal context. But it still, nevertheless, was simply never brought up. Ray was going to have

to draw on other things he'd learned, and maybe more important
than what he learned was who he was. He had dreamt about being
in the company of great people. Many with monumental problems.
Many on the verge of a life-changing event. Better people than him.
So often was the case that he just listened, and that helped him
learn something extremely important. He learned that sometime,
even most of the time, listening was the greatest gift you could give
to people. People were smart in certain ways, even the dodo's that
didn't know about history, the way Ray did. Didn't know the Bill of
Rights, or God-forbid, who the allies were during World War Two,
and who the Axis Powers were. People were smart enough to know
that usually, you couldn't fix their problems, and the bigger their
problems were, the less likely you would be able to change it. Less
likely to do anything about it. Ray could listen. He liked to talk, too.
That was the easy part. His Mom would say "God gave you just one
mouth but two ears for a reason." "Corny, Mom", Ray would say, but
there was great truth to it. But Ray had a bigger problem. Listening,
he could do, but what about advice? What about answers to a
problem he had no clue about. NO DAMN CLUE! He hadn't lived it,
didn't know what it felt like. Day in, day out, like a hammer chipping
small pieces of stone off a great statue, except this time, chipping
small pieces off a person's being. Their soul. Their individuality.
Their self-purpose. How was Ray supposed to deal with something
like that? To answer it. He had his own misunderstandings about
this very subject. He didn't understand it. Didn't know how it came to
be? But, did he understand John Adams, Neil Armstrong? People in
a different place and time? But this wasn't a different place or time,
and it wasn't the same thing, and it wasn't a famous person. This
person, this young man named Todd, would likely NEVER be
famous. Who was to know, but what did that even mean? Is being
famous a requirement for happiness? Are you anything less
because you aren't famous? Do you deserve less in life? Ray
instinctively knew that the answer was no. That's it. Instinct. Did Ray
have to be trained in consulting others? Could he simply be a
decent human? Decency and dignity. His Dad used it a lot, to
describe history. Always history, something famous. "Well, dad, Dr.
Gene, no everything and everybody is famous, so now what?
Dignity, decency. Ray read "How to Win Friends and Influence
People" once a year. His Dad pressured him to read it. He was
reluctant. It wasn't history, wasn't a space story, it was a "self-help"

book. "No, his dad said". It was a book about understanding people, about dealing with people. "Boring", thought Ray. His Dad had to find a portion of the book in which Abraham Lincoln wrote a very critical letter to a General, about his poor leadership on the battlefield. For Lincoln, it was scathing. But many years later, after Lincoln's assassination at Ford's Theater, by John Wilkes Booth, that letter was found, among other possessions of Lincoln's. It was never sent. Lincoln must have realized that the letter would have done little to help the General find redemption. To help him face his problem and come out the other end a better person. Perhaps it was an exercise for Lincoln. Therapy.

No, Ray wasn't an expert in human rights, a trainer, a therapist, not even a historian in this subject, like he liked to think of himself in other areas. Nevertheless, he couldn't just listen. He would have to help Todd, but what could he say? Again, the words kept returning. Decency, dignity. What else, what other words could Ray draw upon? What had he learned that he could apply to somebody who needed help, needed comfort, needed strength, a reason to have hope and go on, when Ray simply hadn't walked in this person's shoes? He kept thinking, but he had better think fast.

"Walk in another person's shoes". Ah, ever the movie buff, especially historical movies, Ray recalled watching "To Kill a Mockingbird, by Gregory Peck". In that movie, his character, Atticus Finch, explained something of importance to his daughter, Scout:

"You never really understand a person until you consider things from his point of view… until you climb in his skin and walk around in it."

Of course, as good as the movie was, and it was a great movie (what Gregory Peck movie was ever bad, thought Ray), the book by Harper Lee, from "next door" in Alabama, was even better, and drew upon her own experiences of bigotry and injustice in the south. A Stone man was put on trial for a rape that he never committed.

Only three months earlier, Ray and two of his friends saw the movie "The Boys from Brazil", again, starring Gregory Peck, as a Nazi. Now, THIS caught Ray's interest, being the World War Two enthusiast, he was. Gregory Peck as a modern-day Josef Mengele. What a great actor! Ray hated him, and that's why he loved him. In that movie, there was a gruesome scene where three Doberman Pinchers attack a man. In the University of Georgia theater crowd, a voice rang out "How 'bout dem Dawgs", the Georgia slogan, and the crowd went crazy. Yes, the "dogs" won that day.

Dignity and decency. Everybody deserved it. Ray didn't have to understand everybody's problem to apply fundamental human rights to a situation. He couldn't cure Lou Gehrig of ALS and he had no understanding of what it felt like. Be a person, Ray. Apply what you know. Listen, but then apply what you know, what people have told you. Greater people than you. Respect, pride, dignity, decency. Face you own fears, your own prejudices, your own ignorance, to do what's right. Maybe this wasn't just about Todd. Maybe it was a test for himself. Ray didn't know, but he knew that he had to do something.

"Look, Todd. You and I, we're strangers. I don't have a lot of friends, really. I withdraw into my books, but I don't have the problems you have. I don't have the knowledge, the intelligence, but I have leaned some things, been taught some things, and maybe some things are just instinct. Some things I was just born with. People go through difficult situations that they didn't cause. Sometimes, they are punished for who they are, and they are good inside. They have to persevere. You're a good person. I can tell that already, even though I haven't spent more than a few minutes around you. I don't know why you are the way you are, but certainly, you're not alone. People are afraid to speak out. Maybe someday, it will be different. I have read about people about to die. I don't know what happens when you die, but today, you're alive, and I've read that as long as you're alive, there's hope. You're wrong about something very, very big." "What's that", said Todd. Ray continued. "Your life IS worth living. If you can't believe you're a person of worth, think about the good you can bring to others." "Think of others?" asked Todd. It was said partly in anger, partly in sorrow, and partly in confusion. "Yes", said Ray. "Think of the value you can give to others. In work, yes, but more importantly, how your pain can be shared, how you can bring your experience in life to others. In friendship, maybe in love." Ray wasn't sure where this was coming from. "Maybe your time to shine isn't now. You've got to hang in there. Maybe it will be around the corner. You know, in a year, just like me, you'll be out of high school, away from the halls of Cedar Shoals High". In college, maybe you'll find your freedom, people with your interests. Certainly, people with your love of science and computers. Maybe people with other interests, other things that interest you. A year or two away, that's all. I can't promise you that you'll find everything you need next year, or the year after, but you must go on. Things DO change, one way or another. You're worth a lot, Todd. Think of the possibilities. Keep that Ray of hope alive". "Funny", said Todd, forcing a smile. Ray realized his pun. "Well, I'm no expert". "That's for sure", said Todd. "You're sounding more like a member of my family every day, with the sarcasm", Ray smiled. "You can't quit now" Ray said. Society changes, but you must find your happiness now. Find it within yourself.

Ray felt he had Todd "hooked" on the value of sarcasm to show affection, warmth, or caring, if done correctly. Todd was "getting it". "Look, even though you're attending the 'North Avenue Trade School' (the term rival Georgia students gave to Georgia Tech, located on that Atlanta Avenue), I'll allow you to be my friend. My token GA Tech friend, and my token gay friend. That was the test. Todd laughed. Years later, this was to be the "cement", the cornerstone of their friendship. School rivals, gay vs straight jokes. They made it work because they developed trust and understanding. Words that might have hurt Todd before, that DID hurt him, that cut him, were now being reversed in their meaning, to show affection, to show that these words were not going to have the same affect that they did before. He would be hurt again, by life, by ignorant people, by people who didn't understand the importance, the value, the necessity of dignity, but now, Ray had helped, at least somewhat, to fight back. It wasn't a monumental breakthrough. That would be too easy, too simple. A mockery. No, it was a glimmer, it was small but meaningful. Something, maybe to build upon. What is that? In theory, it was simple. Todd was a person, a human, made the way he was by God, or nature, or something. Who knows? Ray wasn't sure, but there Todd was. A person. More than just a person. A nice guy. A guy who didn't need changing. Ray's parents would always say "just be yourself". His Mom, in her rare display of comedy, would add, "be yourself, but a version of yourself that picks up your dirty underwear off the floor". "Thanks, Mom" Ray thought. There's always time for a parent to lay on a little embarrassment.

It was so simple. Todd wasn't out of the woods. To be clear, he would NEVER be out of the woods. Even as he grew older, found his niche, a career. He still faced prejudice. It never went away. No, it never went away. But he found people to surround himself with. People who shared his passions, in more ways than one. People to admire. People to love. It wasn't so simple for Ray, either. He had his prejudices to deal with. No matter how hard he tried, his own misunderstandings about Todd, his feelings, his life, were things he would think about. But he realized that he didn't HAVE to understand everything. Things confused him. Even made him uncomfortable. He understood enough, perhaps. Decency, dignity. Now, friendship.

Ray said "Todd, I want you to write my number down, and I'll take yours. I want you to meet my family. Come over for dinner. You'll like my family. Even my sister. Linda is in 10th grade and something of a math genius. I could see her going to Tech if she doesn't go to MIT or Harvard, and look, you'll have to start trusting somebody again. I'll call you tomorrow. It's 12:30 and I'm already in trouble.

They swapped phone numbers, although stay could see that the trust wasn't completely there. It had been broken too many times and trust took time to build. They were still strangers but I time, this evening would be recalled as a very special event. Another "event" for Ray, but a lasting one, a real one.

"Todd, you CAN go home tonight, right?" "Yes, I can go home. I wasn't kicked out. I just don't want to go home." "Then you have to go home", and Todd did. Ray caught a break. He got home at 12:50 and everybody was asleep. Nobody knew the difference.

The next day, Ray had a talk with his family. Ray knew his family. Even his sister. "Good for you, Ray", his mom said. Dr. Gene said, "Sure, invite him over for dinner next week". Linda, for once, said nothing.

Ray had to remind himself to call Todd that afternoon. He was a little absentminded. He couldn't forget, and he didn't. "Todd, we'd all like you to come over for dinner next Friday night. Too cold to barbecue, so we're ordering in pizza. Is that okay?" Todd wasn't going to simply fall in line overnight. "What did you tell them about me?" It made no sense to lie, thought Ray. "Everything" said Ray, including that you're a nice guy who likes science a lot, and math, and my sister already wants to trade me for you." "Okay, I'll come", said Todd.

Todd's visit was the first of many to the Stone home, over many years. Todd and Ray learned that they had some good things in common, but other things, not, like anybody else. For one, they both liked the Broadway theater. As Todd picked up on the "Stone sarcasm", he joined in, even spearheaded much of it. "Ray, you're not gay, but you like the theater? Something you want to tell us?" "Hey" said Ray, "a straight guy can't like a good show?" They had a great liking for the show "Oliver", and it became a running joke, whenever Todd showed up at the door. "Hey, everybody" Ray would say to the surprise of nobody. It's Todd! Come on in, Todd!"

"Consider yourself at home
Consider yourself, part of the family
There isn't a lot to spare
Who cares, whatever we've got we share".

Ray would sing this "Oliver" classic in the world's worse cockney accent since Dick VanDyke. "Mom" screamed Linda. "Make him stop!" But everybody knew the bit was only half over. Todd would come in and together, Ray and Todd would "strut" through the living room, as if on an older London cobblestone street, and continue.

"If it should chance to be
We should see
Some harder days
Empty larder days
Why grouse?
Always-a-chance we'll meet
Somebody
To foot the bill
Then the drinks are on the house!
Consider yourself our mate
We don't want to have no fuss
For after some consideration, we can state
Consider yourself
One of us!"

One day, while both Todd and Ray were in college, and Linda was a high school senior, they were all in town for the holidays. Todd and

Ray decided to go out for a couple of drinks and listen to jet another band trying to make it big from Athens, GA. A couple of beers later, well, more than a couple for Ray, they went back to Ray's house. It was already decided that Todd would spend the night. It was quietly understood that Todd did not stay at his parents any longer.

The rest of the family was watching "It's a Wonderful Life", when the two boys tumbled in. Mom was waiting for their arrival, and apple pie a la mode ready to serve. It was only 9:00 PM.

It was also a little evident that Ray was happy by the time he had gotten home, but he was 20 at a time when the drinking age was 18, and he was home, and everybody was in a festive mood, so "what are you gonna do?" Dr. Gene said nothing.

Ray lifted a cold glass of milk and said, "I want to give a toast". Uh-oh, thought Linda. "What idiotic statement was going to come out of a drunk Ray's mouth?" "Okay" said his Mom, hesitantly, but smiling.

"This is for Todd, who's birthday isn't until January, but it doesn't matter. You know, Todd and I are friends, the same in many ways and yet different in many ways." "Yawn" said Linda, literally. "Get to the pernt, Edith", said Linda again, an "Archie Bunker" reference from "All in the Family".
"Okay!" said Ray. "An eagle and a gazelle are different in many ways, but the same in other ways." "Oh, God" said Lisa. "Forget it, Socrates" she said. Ray continued. "An eagle doesn't understand how a gazelle would run when it could fly among the clouds. On the other hand, the gazelle doesn't understand why the eagle would flap its wings in the air when it could run like wind over hills, through valleys, leap over water, and smell all the wonderful smells in the trees and flowers." "Are you done, old 'Sultan of Sage'?" Todd cracked up and then everybody else did. Even Ray found it funny that Linda pulled that out of the air but kept up his serious appearance. "As I was saying!" Ray feigned annoyance. "They don't always understand each other's ways, but they are both majestic creatures, worthy of praise and awe". Suddenly, a spoonful of vanilla ice cream flew in the air and hit Ray in the face. It came from Todd!! Jeez, Todd!" Shouted Ray, surprised but not upset. "I knew I always liked this guy" laughed Linda. Yes, Todd was part of the family, but he had been for a while.

Ray and Todd would have a lot of talks about a lot of things. Ray considered Todd a close friend now, but Ray could never fully understand Todd's lifestyle. His sexual choice. "Ray, did you choose to be straight? Did you choose how you feel about females?" "No, it's just who I am. Who I've always been". "Bingo" said Todd. "Me too. Do you get it?". "Yes and no". Ray was a work in progress. Imperfect and confused, but he was trying. Todd cut him some slack.

Todd's life would improve at Georgia Tech, as Ray predicted it would, as he expanded his world of contacts. He met more mature students, many who shared his interests and passions. Yes, some that did not, but the taunting, the teasing, went away, if not in society, then on this Atlanta campus, where students were too busy with the demanding coursework. No, there were no clubs for gay students, not yet. Not in 1979, but friendships could be made. Todd learned that he wasn't alone. Ray was a good friend now, but he would be at a different school, and it was okay to have different circles of friends.

It wouldn't get much better for Todd's relationship with his parents. His Mom stayed in contact but seemed distant. Todd's courage while in college grew to where he had a couple of knockdown, drag out fights with his dad, who attended Todd's graduation at Georgia Tech's Grant Field, but then soon after, he and his Dad stopped speaking for years.

Todd excelled in school, and eventually moved to San Jose, CA, where he went to work for a company in Silicon Valley. He became well-off financially. He had failed relationships like everybody. Some lasted, some didn't, but he was mostly happy.

He and Ray never lost touch but were separated by distance and by life. Still, on the rare occasion they would all get together at a home, any home, they'd break out in "Consider Yourself". Many didn't understand the history, but who cared?

One day, Todd's mom called him. His dad was dying from colon cancer. By the time it was discovered, it was already in its final stages and had spread rapidly to other organs. Todd should go see him. "Will he even welcome me?" Todd asked. "It doesn't matter, but I think he wants to see you. Come right away."

Todd visited his Dad at Emory University Hospital. It was awkward. It had been at least six years since they spoke. What should he say? He and Ray had many talks over the years about dignity, love, understanding, and forgiveness. To forgive great hurt was so hard. Todd didn't know if he could forgive his father, but he knew he would never see him again.

"Hi Dad" said Todd. "He can't talk well" Todd's mom said. He's on a lot of pain medication. Why don't you tell him about your job?" his Mom said. Todd talked about his work with a company called "Creative Technology", how he got to travel to Singapore several times a year, and how rapidly the computer industry was changing. He didn't think his mom understood much, and his dad understood nothing. It was empty, meaningless, but on another level, it was important. This was still his dad. Todd was there. They were a family again. Shattered but together.

Todd was at the hospital for an hour. He and his Mom knew that the time was winding down. Todd took a deep breath. "Dad, I don't know if you can hear me or understand, but things have been hard for both of us. It doesn't matter anymore. I love you, and I forgive you." His dad opened his eyes but said nothing. Todd's Mom had tears running down her face. "I love you, too, Mom", and he walked out. Todd's father died two days later at the age of 64. It was 1990, and Todd was 28 years old.

The history of discrimination against the gay community is long in the United States. According to the Associated Press, sodomy laws remained on the books in 13 states as of the middle of 2003. "Sodomy" was illegal for everyone -- gay and straight -- in Alabama, Florida, Idaho, Louisiana, Mississippi, North Carolina, South Carolina, Utah, and Virginia. In addition, four contiguous states, Kansas, Missouri, Oklahoma, and Texas, criminalized certain forms of private, consensual sexual behavior between persons of the same gender, but permitted them if performed by a man and woman.

Homosexual men were sent to concentration camps during World War Two, by the Nazi's, and forced to wear pink triangles.

Gay rights organizations began as early as the 1920s in the United States, but discrimination continued into the 1960s and up to today, although tremendous strides have been made. The AIDS epidemic in the 1980s was a terrible period for many, and in 1992, President Bill Clinton enacted the "Don't ask, don't tell" law so that gay men and women could enter the military, if they hid their sexuality. Advocates did not consider this a victory, and over 12,000 servicemen and woman were kicked out the military for refusing to hide who they were. The law was overturned in 2011.

As late as 1996, Congress passed the Defense of Marriage Act (DOMA), which Bill Clinton signed into law in 1996. The law prevented the government from granting federal marriage benefits to same-sex couples and allowed states to refuse to recognize same-sex marriage certificates from other states.

Massachusetts was the first state to legalize gay marriage, and the first legal same-sex marriage was performed on May 17, 2004—a day when seventy-seven other couples across the state also tied the knot. Gay marriage was finally ruled legal by the Supreme Court in June 2015.

In 2008, Todd Miller was forty-six years old and a successful computer executive. His parents both gone, he lived with his partner just outside of San Jose, and loved to travel whenever possible. California had just allowed same-sex marriages to take place, and Todd and Steven were going to take advantage of it, before somebody changed their mind (which happened, and from November 2008 to 2013, when same-sex couples could not get a license in CA). They had a small ceremony in Monterrey, overlooking the ocean. Just close friends. Ray was one of them. He was the sole representative of the Stone family. Ray and Todd stayed in touch all these years and got together whenever they could. They still joked about the old days. Todd never forgot Ray's kindness, and Ray was thankful that he had Todd as a friend. Todd had helped Ray become a better person. A more understanding, tolerant person.

Ray walked around the private grounds, where you could hear waves crashing against the shore. A cake was on display showing, naturally, two grooms. Ray looked at it. Naturally, it's what Ray would expect to see, but he was still learning, still coping. Maybe his generation, some of them, who grew up in an age of less tolerance, would pause to think. Maybe future generations wouldn't. Ray was happy for Todd.

A young man, who turned out to be Todd's assistant of about 24, walked up to Ray and saw him looking at the cake. "What's wrong, does the cake bother you?" Slightly embarrassed, Ray said "Oh, no, of course not". "Well, I sure hope not", said Todd's assistant. "It looks perfectly normal to me".

SAVAGE CHANTERS

Ray had finished a long day at Allen's, flipping burgers, serving, bussing tables, cleaning, whatever it took to keep the Athens, GA and nearby Navy personnel happy and full. Playing on the radio was a mix of 50s-70s mainstream stuff, sort of all over the place. Ray, on his shift, picked up on pieces of different songs:

- I'll show him that a Cadillac is not a car to scorn. Beep, beep.

- Don't go changing to try and please me. You never let me down before

- My Maserati does 185. I lost my license, now I don't drive

- Father McKenzie, writing the words of a sermon that no one will hear

Ray liked a lot of music. He came from a music town. It might not be Nashville, but Athens, GA had made its mark for its listing of progressive rock bands like the B52s, and R.E.M. Ray still liked "Phil and the Blanks, which he listened to over at T.K. Harty's, which he often got into, even though he was still seventeen. There were ways. He liked the girl bassist, swaying back and forth. He liked it when musicians loved what they were doing. Music with a beat.

Ray liked his music. Rock, pop, maybe a little swing, but not country, and not much of anything else. Oh, Ray liked musicals. Yup, wasn't cool, but he liked the Rogers and Hammerstein stuff, when nobody was around:

"We've got sunlight on the sand
We've got moonlight on the sea
We've got mangoes and bananas we can pick right off a tree
We've got volleyball and ping-pong and a lot of dandy games
What ain't we got?
We ain't got dames!"

Ray would hum, whistle, or just outright sing, when he could get away with it.

Being a lover of college football, he liked college right songs. He was particular and he judged based on melody, regardless of the school. That meant that a rival like Florida and Auburn had fight songs Ray liked, but he kept that quiet. Of course, "On Wisconsin" was his parent's favorite. It was their alma mater. Ray liked it, and the Notre Dame fight song, the Tiger Rag, and he even liked the Tennessee fight song, "Rocky Top", but being a purist, he had to give it a "B", because it sounded more like a country song. But it was peppy. You couldn't deny that.

Many college songs had a certain sound. Ray wasn't a musician, but he knew it when he heard it. A certain structure, certain notes and chords. It followed that structure and didn't venture from it. Ray felt like he could write a college fight song, maybe if he could read music. That would help. But in any event, Ray liked the structure. It was predictable music. Like the game, itself. Line-up, block, open up holes, pass patterns. Things went wrong, went awry, but it was planned. Good athletes could adapt, improvise if necessary, but that certainly wasn't the plan, and a player would have to deal with the wrath of a coach if they didn't follow a play. Coach Dooley might not be too tough on you, but Bear Bryant would probably chew a piece of flesh out of your butt if you didn't do as you were told. Yes, order, planning and structure worked the best in life, in everything you do. There was no doubt that Ray was right.

He finished up a little early, 10:00 PM, because he opened that day, a long, Saturday. It was late January 1979, not too cold, but not much going on, anyway. May as well work. Allen's was a pretty orderly place, but they did serve beer, and once in a while, a couple of guys "got loud", after one too many Budweiser's, and carried on, but Allen's didn't have a bouncer. It never got out of hand. It was more a burger joint than a bar. Ray liked his beer, too. He wondered what the works would be like without it. Without booze. Lower tips, for one thing.

Ray pulled into the driveway at around 10:20, weaving through neighborhoods off of Prince Street. Surprisingly, his parents were out at a party at another Professor's house in Watkinsville, a few miles away. Linda, though, was home, alone, watching an episode of "Fantasy Island". Tattoo, the diminutive sidekick of Mr. Rourke, was yelling "the plane, the plane!" to start each episode. Who would guest start tonight? Like "The Love Boat" and "Love American

Style", there was a steady list of current and past stars. This one had Mary Ann Mobley and Peter Graves, among others, hoping for a certain dream that they would get, only to realize that they were better off without it, and that was the lesson in each story, and in each episode. "Be careful what you wish for". You always knew that the guests would get what they wanted, and then regret it. At least it was predictable.

Linda was lying on the couch., and without missing a beat or looking over at Ray, had a comment, as usual. "Oh, you're home. I could smell the grease." "Yup, my grease," answered Ray. "The smell of a working man, instead of chips and cookies, the smell of a lazy couch potato. Say, has Mr. Rourke and Tattoo granted you your fantasy, yet?" Linda answered, "No.....you're still here." Ray had to laugh. It was quick. Gotta hand it to her, Linda was sharp. She was predictable.

Ray took a much-needed shower. Linda was at least partially right about the grease. A long, hot shower and then some Saturday Night Live.

Tonight's Saturday Night Live featured Monty Python's Michael Palin and musical guest The Doobie Brothers. The Doobies performed "What a Fool Believes" and "Takin' it to the Streets". Ray loved the Doobies, led by Michael McDonald, and loved the hard-charging' 2nd song lyrics:

"You don't know me but I'm your brother
I was raised here in this living Hell
You don't know my kind in your world
Fairly soon, the time will tell
You, telling me the things you're gonna do for me
I ain't blind and I don't like what I think I see"

John Belushi did a samurai skit, and it was always funny to hear Dan Aykroyd say "Jane, you ignorant slut", and Ray dosed off just before the ending credits.

Suddenly, Ray awoke, standing before steps to a home. It was a large, older house, with a lot of music coming from it. Jazz music. He looked behind him, and he saw in the dark, a street sign that said, "Camp Street". Ray walked up the stairs toward the door, and suddenly, it swung open, a puff of smoke drifting out, and the music much louder.

"Well, well, we got ourselves a nice bimbo, don't we?" It was a cute girl, not much older than Ray, wearing a skirt with fringes on it, and wearing a string of beads over a white blouse. Ray had no idea what she was talking about. "A bimbo?" Ray repeated. Not angrily, just curious. "Well, sure", she said. "Got yourself an invitation?" Ray was totally lost. "Well, I"

He was interrupted. "You're not a gatecrasher now". Ray could only say, "Oh, no, I just." She broke in again. "Oh, come on. A cake eater like you? I'm not a dumb Dora! I'm Helen" as she laughed at her cleverness, "C'mon in honey!"

Ray walked in. "So, honey, who are you?" "Oh, I'm Ray", he said, trying desperately to get a grip of his surroundings. Clearly, a party, lots of music, booze, that's for darned sure, much of it consumed by Helen. That was also pretty certain.

"Hey, Ray-Jay", Helen said, how about a little giggle water?" Ray had no idea, but he had little to lose here. "Sure". "Ducky!" said Helen. They walked through the house, people laughing and loud jazz music. Ray was handed a glass of liquid. "Okay", thought Ray. Booze. That's what he figured.

"Oh, Vet!" Helen shouted. "Your friend Ray is here!" Helvetia Boswell approached Ray.

"Well, hello, stranger" said Helvetia, but Vet to her friends. "Well, you see..." Ray tried to explain. Vet ignored Ray's explanation. "Glad you're here, Mr. Ray", she said, faking formality. "Helen looks like you've gotten into the hooch, there".

"Ah, don't be a flat tire, Vet." laughed Helen. Ray couldn't keep up. Helen turned to Ray and whispered, "Helen's a little ossified!" "I can see" said Ray. What it meant, he didn't know, but if it meant drunk, then yes, Helen was ossified. Helen said "Hey, Vet, I'll leave you alone with the big cheese while I go take a powder" and waked down the hallway.

Suddenly, an older looking girl walked up to the two of them and said, "Well, Vet,

who's this young man?" "Martha Boswell, this is my friend, Ray". With Vet's announcement of Ray as her friend, and the "hooch flowing freely, Ray was in. He was SOMEBODY'S friend. There would no issues. "You know my sister, Martha?" Said Vet. Ray didn't know if it was a question or a statement. "Yes", well, I know all about you", said Ray, but he knew nothing. "Hey, Martha, scram" said Vette, mockingly. I saw him first!"

"Hey, you two, let's go!" came a voice from the "parlor", or "living room", which was a large room with a piano setup. On the side, Ray saw some other instruments, a big string base, guitar, clarinet, against the wall. "We've got some singing to do, Ray", Martha said. "Have some fun and stick around awhile." They both got up, and then Vette turned around and said "Ray, Helen's a little out on the roof tonight, but she's a good girl." "Certainly", said Ray.

Ray looked over near the front door, and on a small table, he saw a newspaper, finally. His salvation. He glanced down. The Times-Picayune, Saturday, January 19, 1929. Well, that explained a lot. The speech, the booze, illegal at the time, the music, the clothing Thank God for newspapers to at least get Ray into the right century and year. He hadn't left the 20th century, but he certainly left the confines of 1978 Athens, GA. It seemed that both cities did have one thing in common. New Orleans was a haven for music, but not the kind of music that Ray listened to, or even understood.

Around the well-light home, he saw people of different ages, and to his great surprise, white and Stone guests, walking around, laughing, and all of them drinking. Smoking, too. At one point he heard somebody one guest say to another "butt me", and out came a pack of cigarettes.

The three young women huddled around a piano, the two Ray had met, Vette, and Martha, joined another young woman who was seated at the piano. The seated woman was Connee, Connie Boswell, and the three together formed the singing Boswell Sisters, and this was their home. Vette was only seventeen, the same age as Ray, while Martha was 23, and Connee, 21.

Then, Connee started playing a slow tune, all alone at first:

"Now I've been having 'em, been having 'em all day long
I got the jeebies, but I can't go wrong
Cause when I got them, I just roll along
Now listen everybody while I sing this song"

She sang a couple of verses, and then the most incredible thing happened, at least to Ray. The music got much faster, and the three Boswell Sisters, Martha, Connee, and Vette, started singing in harmony, but it was like it was one person singing. Now are they doing that? Ray had yet to really experience what was called "close harmony". Oh, sure, The Beach Boys sounded great, but this was precision, but in a way, it wasn't. It was loose, kind of all over the place, but then it got more so after the next verse:

"Oh... skeet scat
A-doodle-lat, a-loodle-lat
A doodle-lat boe, ba-dump-a
A-laddle-lat-bum, a laddle-lat bum
A whoo-wat doo, a whoodle-lat-doo"

Why, that was scat. "C'mon Ray!" He could hear Helen saying, "Don't be such a flat tire!". Ray liked it. In a way, it had precision but, in another way, it didn't at all. It was kind of a controlled chaos, but one thing was certain. The Boswell Sisters, or "Bozzies", as he heard through the night, knew what they were doing. The crowd sure loved it!

The song ended and the crowd cheered for more. "Well, as long as we're still waiting for our special guests, we'll do another, but we're gonna need some help." She looked at Connee and Vette and got the idea. "Our new friend, Ray, c'mon over here!" Ray thought "Oh, no". "Now c'mon, don't be a flat tire!" The crowd yelled, "Go on, Ray!". Ray had little choice. He walked up, and said to Martha, "I can't sing". Martha said, "Well that's a lot of banana oil, Ray. I'll bet you've got a fine voice, but for now, we just want you to play a cow." "A cow?" asked Ray. "Sure! Down on the ground right here! Down Ray, on all fours". Ray was embarrassed but complied. "Okay", he said, and smiled. "Hey, that's swell! Helen, you're our farmer! C'mon over here", and Martha placed a chair next to Ray. "Well, hello, handsome" said Helen. Helen already knew the bit. The Bozzies started singing while Helen pretended to "milk" Ray.

"Milk, beautiful milk
C'mon cutie and do your duty,
Give, cow, give
Stop denying us, start supplying us
Give, cow, give
You know, the hens lay eggs
And the sheep give wool
Everybody's doing their bit
Cow don't be a Bolshevik"

It was innocent. I mean, after all, the Bozzies parents and several older jazz lovers were there. It could have gotten far more interesting, especially given Helen's nature, but she kept her hand under Ray's stomach, presenting to milk a cow.

With the song over, the Bozzies said "Now how about a hand for Helen and Ray, and no raspberries, now!" Ray the now as welcome as another round of giggle juice. He may as well have been a first cousin that lived next door. Even the hooch was tasting pretty good, but Ray told himself that this was the 2nd and final glass. What was in this stuff, who knows.

Prohibition in the United States was a nationwide constitutional ban on the production, importation, transportation, and sale of alcoholic beverages from 1920 to 1933. Prohibitionists first attempted to end the trade in alcoholic drinks during the 19th century.

The 3 goals of Prohibition were 1) Eliminate drunkenness and the resulting abuse of family members and others. 2) Get rid of saloons, where prostitution, gambling, and other forms of vice thrived. 3) Prevent absenteeism and on the job accidents stemming from drunkenness.

It didn't work, not in the U.S, not in New Orleans, and not on Camp Street. While the 18th Amendment began the prohibition of alcohol, its proponents called the "dry's", it only advanced the sale of illegal alcohol sales, private clubs known as "speakeasy's", and criminal activity. There were said to be up to 100,000 speakeasies in New York City alone.

Opposition to Prohibition grew every year, and finally overturned with the passage of the 21st Amendment signed into law by Franklin Delano Roosevelt.

Suddenly, the door swings open, and a smiling Stone man entered with three other men. Mrs. Boswell yelled out. "Louis!" The Stone man in front, displayed the widest grin that Ray had ever seen, and shouted in a gravelly voice "Louis is here!" A shout or two or "Satch" and "Pops" was heard. "And I got the whole 'Hot Five' boys with me". That would include second: Fred Robinson on trombone, Jimmy Strong on clarinet and tenor saxophone, Earl Hines on piano, Mancy Carr on banjo, and Zutty Singleton on drums.

"Well, ain't that the berries!" Yelled Vette, and Martha ran up and hugged Louis, only 28 years old, but the most famous jazz performer in America. Connee smiled from ear to ear, and Louis walked quickly to the piano and gave Connee a big, Louie Armstrong hug. Louis, as well as everyone else, knew that Connee had contracted polio as a young girl, and couldn't walk.

The entire Boswell family knew Louis Armstrong. The Boswell Parents would hear him on steamboats in New Orleans. As a younger girl herself, Mrs. Boswell would sneak out to the infamous "Red Light District" known as "Storyville". Louis followed his mentors, cornet player Joe "King" Oliver, and trombonist Edward "Kid" Ory. Louis followed the King to Chicago, where his fame grew.

"Satchmo'" given that nickname for his large mouth, resembling a satchel, wrote Mrs. Boswell, telling her that he was coming back to New Orleans for only a week, before heading to New York. He was to play in the orchestra for a new show, "Hot Chocolates" an all-Stone review, so Mrs. Boswell knew he was coming that night, and thought how fun it would be to surprise her daughters and guests, but Louis kept an equally big surprise.

"No, cutting now," Connee told Louis, and Louis gave out a huge laugh. It was infectious. Ray might not know jazz, but the world knew Louie Armstrong. "Ha Ha" Louis yelled with delight, and hugged Connee again. "Cutting" helped make Louis famous. It was the practice of "cutting in" to another band's session, to out-play. Even the talented Boswell Sisters wouldn't want to compete with the "Hot Five".

Suddenly, a young white man walked through the door. The guests stopped in their tracks. It couldn't be. Ray didn't understand. It was a rather normal-looking man in a nice suit. Perhaps 30ish.
"I'm just clammed", Vette said softly.

"Well, hello," said the well-dressed man. Don't let me bust up this swell shindig. It was the one and only Hoagy Carmichael, a friend of Louis', and himself ready to setup shop in New York. One correspondence led to another, and Hoagy made us his up to Chicago, and the entire gang came down to New Orleans for a week, before travelling to New York.

Hoagy Carmichael, was an Indiana University graduate, and law school graduate as well, but the law wasn't his calling. In 1927, Carmichael wrote and recorded one of the great standards in American songwriting history, "Stardust", and everybody knew it. Even Ray would have heard it, somewhere. "Hello, Mrs. Boswell. Louis has told me so much about you and your talented daughters". Meldania Boswell couldn't believe her good fortune. Always a music lover, with her husband himself a vaudeville performer, she and her husband introduced their son, Clydie, known as "Clydie" and three daughters to classical music in the New Orleans area. Clydie, their only son, died of influenzas at nineteen, and 1918, but their daughters caught the jazz bug and began touring through several states. By 1925, the Boswell Sisters had already recorded their own record, and would set out again later in 1929.

This "jazz-fest" was turning out to be a collection of jazz greats. Louis and his Hot Five were here. That alone was historic, but Hoagy Carmichael was just not expected. Vette's friend, Louis Prima, just nineteen, and also a trumpet player and New Orleans native was at the party with him Mother Boswell friend, Angelina. Together, they would visit the Stone, and the Italian clubs around New Orleans, and their children all grew up to become well-known jazz artists. Louis formed his own band as early as 1924, when he was fourteen years, and was only a few months away from joining another New Orleans jazz band, and getting married, all before the age of twenty.

Mrs. Boswell, clearly used to famous musicians, was nevertheless overtaken with the famous Hoagy Carmichael, turned to Louis Armstrong and said "Oh, Louis, you little rascal", and Louis gave out a loud laugh. "Yes, we schlepped 'ole Hoagy away from his Indianapolis law firm". "Schlepped?" thought Ray. Yes, Louis Armstrong was befriended and helped by the Karnofsky family, right in New Orleans, and he spoke fluent Yiddish. It was said that he wore a Star of David for his entire adult life.
Mrs. Boswell proudly walked Louis and Hoagy around the room, many whom knew them personally, anyway, especially Satchmo, though everybody knew Hoagy Carmichael. Ray was near the piano, sitting in a chair, when Vette, figuring she was doing Ray a huge favor by introducing him to these famous jazz musicians said, "Louis, this our friend, Ray." "Well, hello there, Ray" Satchmo said. "If you're a friend of the Bozzies, then you're a friend of mine, oh yeah!" Everybody laughed. Hoagy said, "So Ray, you live in the

neighborhood?" Nobody had asked a lot of details about Ray, and he thought he had this issue beat. He decided he'd better let some truth come out. "Well, I'm from Georgia". Nobody really blinked, but Hoagy raised his eyebrows, slightly. "Georgia? You don't say. I've been tossing a song idea around about Georgia. Yes, Georgia has been on my mind, lately." The statement caught the attention of absolutely nobody.

"Hey, we've got too much talent around here to waste it. Get up there, Louis". Why, I thought you'd never ask!" Drums and instruments were setup in the corner, next to the piano, and the Hot Five belted out a couple of tunes.

Louis and his band began by playing the haunting Saint James Infirmary, where, as often was the case, Satchmo both played the trumpet and sang:

"I went down to St. James Infirmary
Saw my baby there
She was stretched out on a long white table
So cold, so sweet, so fair

Let her go, let her go!
God bless her wherever she may be
She can look this wide world over
But she'll never find a sweet man like me"

A "Basin Street Blues" and the iconic, "West End Blues", the Hot Five took a break, and the crowd shouted for Hoagy, who played Stardust, due to popular demand, and a new song not yet recorded until 1930, called "Up a Lazy River".

After that, it was one artist after another, as if everybody in the house, with the possible exception of Ray and Mrs. Boswell, played in one way or another. Ray did his best to mingle with the guests, relying on his talent for listening, which seemed to work at any time in history. "Hi, I'm Ray. Tell me about yourself" was usually all he needed to do. Performers about to go out on the road, joining a band, trying to make music their full-time job, even personal problems. A little bit of giggle juice, and people were always up to talking about themselves.
Ray was new to this music, but he seemed to be right in the middle of history, in a single home. It was hard to believe.

It might be said that jazz originated in New Orleans at the turn of the 20th century, were African, French, Caribbean, Italian, German, Mexican, American Indian and other backgrounds helped form the music. Early jazz also incorporated church hymns, slave songs, field chants, and Cuban-style rhythm. However, jazz didn't get its big break until the 1890s when "ragtime", a precursor to jazz, started to catch the ear of white Americans. The most famous of the artists at the time was Scott Joplin who composed forty-four original ragtime pieces before his death in 1917. It was around this time that other artists started to add in improvisation to the sound, a crucial component of what would become modern jazz.

Improvisation is what made jazz largely what it is. The freedom that came even as early as the end of Civil War, played a part. It was a combination of harmonic melodies from Europe with the upbeat tempo and beats of Africa and other lands. Improvisation was a talent derived from practice and skill and was more a variation on the theme than a total departure from the theme. You had to still adhere to the melody, the harmonics, you could stray, but had to stay honest to the song. Ray wasn't sure he could understand. Years later, Jazz artist Wynton Marsalis would say *"In Jazz, improvisation isn't a matter of just making any ol' thing up. Jazz, like any language, has its own grammar and* vocabulary. *There's no right or wrong, just some choices that are better than others."*

After Ray decided to try "just one more" glass of "homemade punch". He saw Louis wiping his perspiring forehead with a handkerchief. "Excuse me, Mr. Armstrong". "Mr. Armstrong? Ain't no Mr. Armstrong around here, my friend", I'm Louis, and he laughed out loud. Ray thought. "How can anybody not like this man, I mean, not adore him?" "Sorry, Louis". "Ha ha", Louis said, "It's all berries". "Well Louis, what IS jazz, exactly?" Louis laughed, like Ray saw him do again and again that night. "If you have to ask what jazz is, you'll never know." "Well," said Ray. "Whatever it is, I like it, and I like your playing". "Yeah, yeah", said Satchmo. Well thank you, my good man!" and or course, smiled and laughed some more, and Ray hadn't even seen him drink any "giggle juice."

The night began to draw to a close, and it was 1:30 AM, late even for Ray, but seemingly, not so late for this crowed. Many of the musicians here would be moving out of New Orleans, some to Chicago, many, like the "Hot 5" and Hoagy, to New York, where gigs were waiting. Many to Los Angeles, where Hoagy would eventually settle and add acting to his repertoire. "THAT'S where I've seen him!", thought Ray, the movie and World War Two buff. "It's Butch, the piano player, from 'The Best Years of Our Lives'" Yes, Ray was right, he played Butch in the Frank Capra classic about returning servicemen from World War Two.

As the stock market crashed, and the depression set-in, the heyday of jazz has away to big band music, and groups like the Andrew Sisters, another close-harmony group, took center stage, as did Benny Goodman, Gene Krupa, Harry James, Glenn Miller, and Tommy Dorsey.

Jazz artists are still revered, and the craft still practiced. The all-stars of jazz included Louis, Duke Ellington, John Coltrane, Thelonius Monk, Charlie Parker, Wes Montgomery, Ella Fitzgerald, Count Basie, Wynton Marsalis, Chet Baker, and others.

Jazz wasn't for everybody, even at its height. The Boswell sisters, in a matter of months after this party, headed out to Los Angeles. They appeared on radio programs, recorded music for films, and made several recordings. Their unique approach did not always sit well with listeners.

In their first year of radio broadcasting in California, many of the listeners complained at their freestyle way of phrasing songs: "Why don't you choke those Boswell Sisters? How wonderful it would be if they sang just one song like it was written. Really when they get through murdering it, one can never recognize the original." Another outraged letter from an angry listener read: "Please get those terrible Boswell Sisters off the station! You can't follow the melody and the beat is going too rapidly. And to me they sound like savage chanters!"

"Well, Ray, don't want to give you the bum's rush, but we're calling it a night". Vette said, "Oh, yeah, I guess it's time for me to go". "We loved meeting you, and Vette gave Ray a peck on the cheek. Helen did better than that, "Ray, you are just the cat's meow", and planted a kiss right on Ray's lips. Ray was embarrassed but acted as if it happened all the time. It was something he'd remember for a long, long time.

"Goodbye, everybody. It was the bee's knees!" Ray felt like an idiot, but the girls smiled and waved. When in Rome.

Ray left the Boswell home to an empty Camp Street and headed south, for no reason at all. He just had to let things take its course. The weather was on the cold side, and no wonder, as it was 2:00 AM. He found himself on Louisiana Avenue, and after a few blocks, there it was, seen only in books and movies for Ray, the mighty Mississippi. Ray had always wanted to see it, as a student of geography as well as history. He wondered how many songs must have been written about the Mississippi River. He wasn't sure, as it still wasn't his genre, but the list was long, and included Can you Canoe, Muddy Waters, Old Man River, Waiting on the Robert E. Lee, and many more.

From northern Minnesota to the Gulf of Mexico, the Mississippi was America's longest river, and soon, after flowing through New Orleans, it would empty into the Gulf of Mexico, after a journey of 2,230 miles.

Ray saw a barge making its way north on the river, and he sat down on a bench along the riverbank. He never knew what was in that hooch he was drinking, but he hoped it was the "good stuff", considering the source. He was exhausted, but his head back on the bench, and was out in a few minutes.

Ray woke up as he almost always did, staring at the University pennants on the wall from Wisconsin and Georgia. He had somewhat of a headache as he headed downstairs to a waiting breakfast table.

"Hey, look what the cat dragged in", said an ever-loving Linda, his kindly sister. "Hey, I worked, what's your excuse". "Aren't we touchy, said, Linda". Ray said to his parents, "So, I got back from Allen's at 1:00, and you two weren't even home, yet". "Uh, Ray", said Dr. Gene. "I didn't know we had a curfew" he said, mostly tongue-in-cheek. "Fact is" Ray's Mom said' "It was you dad's fault". He got into a, let's say, spirited discussion on history, and then music, with Dr. Peterson." "Yeah", said Dr. Gene. "The authority on everything". "Well," said Carol, "You had your strong opinions, too". She turned to Ray and Linda, "A few drinks helped out with that". "DAD", said, Linda. "Shame". "Dr. Gene was not much of a drinker. It was probably two drinks and besides, thought Ray, it took very little arm-twisting to get his Dad into a debate on the history of virtually anything. I mean, that was, after all, his trade. "Ah", said, Ray. "A little too much of the ole' giggle juice, huh?" His parents laughed, "Where did you come up with THAT word?" said his Mom. "From a book", Linda said. "A book for idiots". "Ah, close your head", said Ray. Linda had no idea what in the world that meant, but rather than say anything else, she completed their daily little insult-fest, not with a word, but with a hand gesture that would probably have worked in 1929 as it did in 1978.